*Harlequin Romance® is thrilled to
present another wonderful book from
award-winning author*

Liz Fielding

*Liz Fielding will keep you captivated
for hours with her contemporary,
witty and feel-good romances.*

RITA® Award-winning author Liz Fielding
"gets better and better with every book!"
—*Romantic Times BOOKclub*

VG Story Liked it
No S Better then most
of her books
One of her
best

Dear Reader,

Some books spring from our own experiences, needing nothing more than the well of memory and imagination to fill the pages. Others are driven by ideas that require much research: reading any number of fascinating books, delving about on the Internet, sending impertinent e-mails to total strangers who respond with amazing patience and kindness. Fleur Gilbert's story falls into the second category.

Whilst I understood the basics of plant breeding, I am eternally grateful to Clare Green at the Royal Horticultural Society (www.rhs.org.uk), Derek Luther at the British Fuchsia Society (www.thebfs.org.uk) and Bob Hall at the Ammanford Fuchsia & Pot Plant Society for many of the details I used in this book. I am also indebted to the Web site of the Stroke Association (www.strokeassociation.org).

Any errors are my own.

With love,

Liz

THE FIVE-YEAR BABY SECRET

Liz Fielding

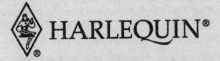

TORONTO • NEW YORK • LONDON
AMSTERDAM • PARIS • SYDNEY • HAMBURG
STOCKHOLM • ATHENS • TOKYO • MILAN • MADRID
PRAGUE • WARSAW • BUDAPEST • AUCKLAND

ISBN 0-373-03893-3

THE FIVE-YEAR BABY SECRET

First North American Publication 2006.

Liz Fielding started writing at the age of twelve, when she won a writing competition at school. After that early success there was quite a gap—during which she was busy working in Africa and the Middle East, getting married and having children—before her first book was published in 1992. Now readers worldwide fall in love with her irresistible heroes, and adore her independent-minded heroines. Visit Liz's Web site for news and extracts of upcoming books at www.lizfielding.com.

Books by Liz Fielding

HARLEQUIN ROMANCE®
3853—HER WISH-LIST BRIDEGROOM
3872—A NANNY FOR KEEPS
3885—THE MARRIAGE MIRACLE

PROLOGUE

FLEUR GILBERT hesitated on the registry office steps. This was not how her wedding day was meant to be.

She should have spent the morning being fussed over by her mother, laughing and crying, remembering all the stupid things she'd ever done. Her friends should have been there, the girls she'd known all her life. She wanted Sarah, a posy of little bridesmaids in frilly frocks.

Bells should be ringing in the village church where her parents had been married, as had countless generations of Gilberts before them.

She should be dressed in white with her father at her side, squeezing her hand to give her courage, to tell her that she was the most beautiful bride ever; proud and happy and hiding a tear as he gave away his little girl to some man who couldn't possibly be good enough for her.

But she was marrying Matthew Hanover and their wedding could never be like that. She knew Matt was right. This was the only way, but, locked inside their private world, insulated by a love so intense, so perfect that nothing and no one else had seemed to matter, she had overlooked the reality of what today would be like.

'Not having second thoughts, are you?' She looked up at

the man she loved, for one blissful moment believing that he was seeing this from her point of view. Had, at the last minute, recognised how far from her dreams this day must be.

But he was smiling. Joking to cover his own nerves.

'No,' she said. 'No, of course not.'

His smile faltered. 'I'd be happier if you sounded a little more confident.'

She shook her head, smiled and leaned against him.

Her first thought on meeting Matthew Hanover face to face, seeing beyond his name, had been that this was it. That he was the one. Nothing had changed that.

'I'm not having second thoughts about you, Matt. I'm just not looking forward to telling either of our families what we've done.'

'What can they do? A month from now we'll be working far away from Longbourne.'

'I suppose so.'

'Whatever happens we'll be together, Fleur, man and wife.' His hand closed protectively over hers. 'Nothing our families do will ever be able to change that.'

CHAPTER ONE

'HAS the post come?'

Fleur paused to scoop up the bills, catalogues and other mail scattered over the doormat, then called up the stairs, 'Tom, if you're not down here in two minutes I'm taking you to school just as you are.'

'Slow down, girl. The world isn't going to end if the boy is a minute or two late for school.'

She dumped the mail on the kitchen table beside her father. 'Maybe not, but it's a distinct possibility if I'm late for my appointment with the new bank manager. We need her on-side if we're really going to take this stand at the Chelsea Flower Show.'

He must have caught the uncertainty in her voice, the un-asked question, because he stopped sorting through the mail and, with a certainty she hadn't heard from him in a very long time, he said, 'Yes, Fleur, we really are.'

Then, whatever it took, she'd have to make it happen. Taking a deep breath, she said, 'Right.'

Which made today's appointment even more important.

The retirement of a sympathetic bank manager couldn't have come at a worse time for them. Brian had understood the difficulties of their business, had celebrated their successes

with them and had patiently seen them through the last difficult six years, giving them breathing space, a chance to recover.

She wished she'd been able to do more than fill the bank's
window-boxes to reward his faith in them. Even with every
single thing running on oiled wheels until Chelsea, it was
going to be a huge gamble. She wasn't convinced that her father's health would stand up to the stress of producing show
plants at the peak of condition on a given day in May, but
nothing she could say or do to dissuade him had had any effect. All she could do was try and shield him from financial
worries. Unfortunately, Ms Delia Johnson, the new person at
the bank, had wasted precious little time in writing to invite
them into the office for a 'chat'.

It was concern that their luck was about to run out—actually a cast-iron certainty that the new manager planned to stamp
her own mark on the branch by weeding out accounts that
weren't flourishing—that made her so snappy this morning.

She was going to have to be in top form to 'sell' the business, convince Ms Johnson that it would be in the bank's interest to see them through the additional expense entailed in
mounting an exhibit at the premier horticultural show of the
season.

'Don't fret,' her father said comfortingly, 'you'll be fine.
You might have inherited my green fingers and your mother's
beauty, but thankfully you missed out on our business brains.'
He smiled as he took in the effort she'd made with her appearance. 'You look lovely.'

She knew how she looked. She had to live with her reflection in the mirror; there was nothing she could do about that—
although with no time and less money for visits to the
hairdresser or expensive cosmetics, the likeness to her mother
was less obvious than it might have been—but she'd had to

learn to manage the business the hard way when she'd been tossed in at the deep end. Sink or swim. She was still floundering. It had never been possible to make up the ground lost during that terrible year when her world—all their worlds—had fallen apart.

Her father's lack of interest in the finances of the company, and the discovery that her mother was in the habit of using their capital resources as her own personal piggy bank, had left her out of her depth and swimming against the current.

Even now her father, having said what he thought she wanted to hear, had lost interest, returning to the perusal of the mail. He'd picked up an envelope that, in her rush, she hadn't noticed and her heart sank as she saw the Hanover logo on the envelope.

'Don't they ever give up?' she demanded, glad of a legitimate focus for her anger.

Any other morning she'd have sorted through the post and weeded it out, protecting him from harassment by a hate-filled woman whose sole ambition appeared to be driving them out of business. Out of the village. Off the face of the earth.

'I'd sell out to a developer, let someone build houses on this land, before I'd let Katherine Hanover have it,' she said.

'Chance would be a fine thing. With Katherine on the Parish Council no one is ever going to get planning permission to build on Gilbert land,' her father replied, as calm as she was angry, but then he'd never once got angry.

She wished he would. Rage. Shout. Give vent to his feelings. But he never would say anything bad about the woman. If he still felt sorry for her, she thought, his feelings were seriously misplaced.

'Not when she wants it for herself,' Fleur said bitterly.

There was a wonderful old barn on the edge of their land

that hadn't been used for anything but storage in years. It was perfect for conversion into one of those upmarket country homes she'd seen featured in the glossy magazines; selling it would have solved a great many of their problems.

The Parish Council, egged on by Katherine Hanover, had decided it was a historic building. They'd not only refused planning permission for conversion, but had warned them that if they allowed it to fall into disrepair they could be fined.

'Maybe I should get involved in local politics,' Fleur said. 'I could at least cancel out the Hanover vote.'

'That would be in your spare time, I suppose,' he said, with a rare smile.

'I could give up doing the ironing,' she said, glad to have amused him. 'It would be a sacrifice, but I could do it.'

'That's better. I thought you were going wobbly on me there for a minute.'

'Who, me? Never.'

As he returned to the letter he was holding, his smile faded as if he didn't have the strength to sustain it. Like his body, it had been worn away under a continual onslaught of betrayal, grief and financial worries, giving her reason—if she needed it—to hate the Hanovers just that bit more.

'Don't open it,' she said. 'Throw it in the bin. I'll shred it and add it to the compost with the rest of them.'

'There have been others?'

Caught out, she shrugged. 'A few. Nothing worth reading.'

'I see. Well, you can do whatever you like with this one since it's addressed to you,' he said, offering her the envelope. 'It appears to have been delivered by hand.'

'By hand?' She reached for it and then shivered, curling her fingers back before they came in contact with the paper. 'Why would Katherine Hanover write to me?'

'Maybe she thinks that you can persuade me to stop throwing her letters away. Maybe she's lost trust in the Royal Mail and that's why she pushed it through the letterbox herself.' Her father seemed to find that as amusing as the thought of Fleur taking up politics. 'It's good to see that she can still get things wrong.' Then he shrugged, dropping the envelope on the table beside her. 'Or perhaps she's offering you a job.'

'Oh, right. That's going to happen.'

'If she's expanding her business she'll need more staff.'

'She's got no room to expand.' With roads on three sides she needed the Gilbert land to extend her empire. 'And why would she need me, anyway? I'm a horticulturist, not a lawn-mower salesman. Hanovers haven't been cultivating their own stock since…since—'

Oh, damn!

'Since your mother ran off with Phillip Hanover?' he finished for her. 'You can say it, Fleur. It happened. Nothing can change that.'

'No.'

In truth, it wasn't the adulterous father but the memory of his faithless son that had caught her unawares. Abandonment was apparently inherent in the Hanover genes, and for a split second she felt a kinship with Katherine.

That was enough to jolt her to her senses.

Katherine Hanover was a vindictive and hateful woman, something that, despite good reason, Fleur was determined not to become.

But it was far better that her father believed she was protecting his feelings than that he should suspect the truth.

'Katherine Hanover would have no use for me, Dad. Not since she paved over her husband's land and turned the business into a gardening hypermarket.'

'True. But she has been advertising for weekend staff for the checkouts in the local newspaper. Maybe she thinks you could do with the money.'

'Whatever would give her that idea?' The grey suit she was wearing—again—that she'd bought for her mother's funeral and had been pressed to within an inch of its life? Or perhaps her go-anywhere black court shoes that had only survived so long because she didn't. Go anywhere, that was.

'Maybe she wants you to see for yourself how much money she's making.'

'You think?' she asked. The new Mercedes, designer clothes, the kind of shoes that provoked envy in every female bosom in the village weren't demonstration enough?

'No, Dad, she's not that stupid,' she said, reaching for the letter, irritated that she could be intimidated at long distance by the woman. 'Just imagine the chaos I could cause in the middle of the weekend rush.' Before she could open it, the clock in the hall began to chime the three-quarters. 'Oh, good grief!' she said, stuffing it into her jacket pocket. 'Tom!'

A five-year-old bundle of energy bounded down the stairs, dog at his heels, and grinning hugely said, 'I'm all ready!'

Her heart caught in her mouth at the sight of him. He'd brushed his hair flat, had tried to fix his tie, which was stuck up almost behind his ear, and his shoes, with their little Velcro tabs, were on the wrong feet.

'I did it all myself,' he said.

'Great job, Tom,' she said, her voice catching in her throat as she picked him up and, despite the need for haste, hugged him until he squeaked and wriggled to be set down. Her little boy was growing up much too fast.

One shoe fell off and, laughing, she picked it up, then sat him on the kitchen table while she straightened him out, scrunching her fingers through his hair to make the curls spring back.

'Don't, Mum!' he said, jumping down, flattening it furiously with both hands. 'Curls are stupid.'

'Sorry,' she said, covering her mouth with her hand, not sure whether she wanted to laugh or cry. Then, 'Have you got everything?'

'Pencil case. Reading book. Indoor shoes. Lunch money.' He went through the daily list, ticking the items off on his fingers.

'What a genius. Do you want an apple for break?' she asked, tucking one into his bag so that she could do a surreptitious check. 'Quick now, give Granddad a hug while I get your coat.'

Matthew Hanover stood at his bedroom window, waiting for Fleur to appear. He hadn't seen her in nearly six years. Not since their wedding night had been disturbed by the soft burble of her mobile phone.

He'd grabbed the wretched thing, determined to switch it off, shut out the world for as long as possible, but she'd seen the caller ID and they'd both known that a phone call from her father in the middle of the night could mean only one thing.

Trouble.

And trouble it had been.

He'd watched, helpless, as the joy, the laughter, had faded from her eyes at the news that her mother had been badly hurt in a road accident. That there was no time to waste.

He'd begged her to let him drive her to the hospital, to be with her, at her side. They were a couple now. Married. But she'd just clung to him for a moment before she'd stepped back and, unable to look at him, had turned away. 'Please, Matt. Not now. My father has enough to cope with.'

And he'd let her go because she was hurting. Because, wrongly, he'd believed it wasn't the moment to fight that battle. He'd let her go with a kiss, trying not to let it hurt that she'd slipped his ring from her finger, saying, 'Call me. Let me know what's happening.'

Then, as if in some dark recess of his mind he'd already sensed the cogs of fate slipping out of sync, he'd gone back to the warm space she'd vacated and had lain in the scent of her body, waiting for her to call.

When his phone had rung half an hour later, though, it hadn't been Fleur. It had been his mother calling to tell him that his father was dead. That Jennifer Gilbert had killed him.

The front door of the Gilbert house opened and a dog, some kind of cross-breed leaning towards a border collie, bounded towards the Land Rover. Then, suddenly, Fleur was there, every inch the businesswoman in a tailored grey suit, her dark red hair swept up into a smooth coil at the base of her neck.

She stood there for a moment, battered briefcase in her hand, her shoulders slumped as if exhausted by the burden she was carrying, and he was glad. She deserved to suffer.

Then she turned as a sturdy little boy raced past her and instinctively his hands went to the window, pressing against the glass as if he could somehow reach out and touch the boy.

How could she have kept that from him?

Denied him his son?

If some anonymous soul hadn't sent him a cutting from the local newspaper with a photograph taken at a performance of the school Christmas Nativity play he might never have known.

One look was all it had taken for him to know that Thomas Gilbert was his son, but to see him in the flesh was something else and pain burned through him like acid as Fleur opened the Land Rover door, her hand hovering at the child's back to give him a boost if he faltered, laughing as he said something to her.

She couldn't have read his letter yet, or nothing on earth would have brought a smile to her lips.

If he'd come home just once. If he hadn't changed the subject whenever his mother had begun her customary whine against the Gilberts...

If, if, if...

There was no point in dwelling on the past. It had taken time to extricate himself from his commitments in Hungary, to transfer the day-to-day running of the agri-business he'd founded there to his deputy. Every day of it had seemed like a year.

The temptation to simply walk away, catch the first flight back to England, had been almost unbearable, but everything had to be properly settled. He'd been determined that no urgent calls for help would distract him from what he had to do, drag him back.

He was here now and ready to make her pay for every one of those five years he'd missed.

She closed the Land Rover door, checking that it was securely shut, sent the dog back inside and shut the door. Then, as she walked round to the driver's side, she paused, turned, as if some faint sound had caught her attention and, spotlit by a weak ray of watery sunlight, she lifted her head and looked up across the boundary fence that divided Gilbert and Hanover land to the window where he was standing. And for a heartbeat he thought she could see him, feel him there, watching her.

But after a moment she turned away and lifted her close-fitting skirt, exposing a yard of leg as she hauled herself up behind the wheel.

'Now, Fleur,' he said softly. *'Now.'*

Fleur dropped Tom off at the school gates just as the bell rang, and he tore off without a backward glance to join his classmates, pushing and giggling as they lined up to go in. Then, as he reached the door, he stopped, turned, looked back and her heart turned over as she caught a reminder of his father. It was in the turn of his head, the lift of his hand, as if he'd been going to wave, but stopped himself just in time in case anyone should see.

She saw it more and more, sometimes held her breath as some old village biddy would look thoughtfully at the boy with a frown, sifting through her memory, trying to recall where she'd seen just that look before. Fortunately, he'd got the distinctive Gilbert colouring, pale red hair that would darken as he grew older, green eyes, rather than the cool grey of his father. So far no one had made the connection, but as the softness faded from the childish cheeks the likeness would become more obvious.

If Katherine Hanover ever suspected…

If only she would move!

Fleur glared at the glossy blue and gold sign that had been erected at the far end of the village where it could be seen from the main road.

Hanovers—Everything For Your Garden.

Fine. She had no quarrel with that, but why here? It would have made so much more sense to have moved to the business park on the other side of Maybridge where they'd fit right in with the Sunday-shopping-as-entertainment venue with its DIY superstores, flat-pack furniture warehouses and giant supermarkets. Where there was plenty of room for expansion. It could only feed the woman's bitterness to live and work next door to a family she seemed to blame for every ill that had ever befallen her.

But then sense had nothing to do with it.

When two families had been rivals in business, and in love, for nearly two centuries, hurting the opposition would always take priority, although it seemed to her that in recent years the Hanovers had caused her family enough grief to satisfy even their capacity for inflicting pain.

She managed to squeeze the Land Rover into a space directly opposite the bank—a good omen, surely—and, having checked her lipstick and tucked a strand of hair in place, she opened the door and crossed the street.

'Goodness, Fleur, I scarcely recognised you,' the receptionist said, buzzing her through.

'Really? Is that good or bad?' she asked.

She rarely applied anything more exciting than the essential sunblock to her skin, but today she'd made the supreme sacrifice in an attempt to impress the new manager with her businesslike image—had put up her hair, added a little style to the hated grey suit with an old silk scarf.

She fiddled self-consciously with one of her earrings, a small swirl of silver studded with a tiny amethyst—her birthstone. Matt Hanover had given them to her instead of a ring the first time he'd asked her to marry him. The first time she'd said, 'Wait. Not now.' Well, she'd been eighteen with three years of college ahead of her. He'd just graduated and was going to the other end of the country to work. Waiting had been the only option. But she'd taken the earrings as a token of his commitment, her promise. And they'd been cheap enough, simple enough to wear openly without her mother cross-questioning her on where they'd come from.

One day, he'd promised her, he'd give her diamonds. She'd laughed, told him she had no need of diamonds when she had him and she'd worn the earrings day and night, certain of his love.

The box, buried in the back of her drawer, had surfaced as she'd searched for a scarf and, unable to help herself, she'd opened it. The stones had perfectly matched the rich purple streaks in the silk and, in a gesture of pure defiance, a promise to herself that neither Hanover—mother or son—had the power to hurt her, she'd fastened them to her ears.

Suddenly, she wasn't so sure.

'You look great,' the receptionist assured her in a whisper as she opened the door. Then, brightly, 'Miss Gilbert to see you, Ms Johnson.'

'Miss Gilbert?' Delia Johnson glanced up from the file in front of her and looked past her to the door. 'Are you alone? I was expecting to see your father.'

Fleur had understood that she wasn't going to be talking to someone who'd known her since she was a baby, someone who knew their history, understood their business. She knew that she'd have to work hard to build a relationship with the new manager.

Ms Johnson, it appeared, wasn't so keen to build a relationship with her.

'He's on file as the sole proprietor,' she prompted.

'That's no longer the case,' Fleur said quickly, ignoring the seat that the woman had waved her towards. 'Our accountant advised creating a formal partnership since my father already leaves most of the business side of things to me these days. He hasn't been terribly well since my mother was killed in a car crash,' she explained.

'Not well? What's the matter with him?'

What could she say? His world had fallen apart, crashed around his ears, and he'd had a breakdown. Had never fully recovered. 'Low grade depression. He copes, but he doesn't go out much. Prefers to concentrate on plant breeding.' Well, it wasn't exactly a secret. 'Brian—Mr Batley,' she corrected, realising that suggesting they were friends might do more harm than good, 'was aware of the situation and was always happy to discuss the account with me.'

'Brian Batley has retired,' Ms Johnson declared, adding something under her breath that sounded like 'and not before time.'

She clearly disapproved of her predecessor's admittedly relaxed attitude and was, no doubt, hell-bent on proving her own management abilities by clearing out businesses which weren't earning their keep.

Gilberts' lack of growth in everything but the size of their overdraft in recent years had probably put them right at the top of her list.

'I assumed that he would have briefed you,' Fleur said. 'Made a note in the file?' Then, realising that might have sounded like a criticism, she quickly added, 'If you'd like to talk to him—my father, that is—you would be welcome to visit the nursery. You could see for yourself what we're doing, although—' she put the briefcase on the chair and extracted a folder '—I have brought along a detailed plan of what we hope to achieve this year.' She placed the folder on the desk. 'You'll see that our major sales drive will be centred around the Chelsea Flower Show,' she began, reconciled to having to educate the woman from scratch about what their business entailed. The time involved in breeding new cultivars, the effort that went into showing—enthused, somehow, with the anticipation, the excitement when there was a major breakthrough. Always assuming that the hard climb up the corporate pole hadn't crushed everything but caution from Ms Johnson's spirit. 'It's been a while since we've shown at Chelsea, but we've been lucky enough to have been offered a stand this year, and we—'

'Later, Miss Gilbert.' Ms Johnson put the folder to one side and opened the file in front of her. 'Please sit down.'

The 'please' was a marginal improvement on her welcome so far, even if it had been less invitation than command. She put her briefcase on the floor, sat down, and when Ms Johnson was sure she had her full attention, she said, 'From the records, Miss Gilbert, it would seem that Brian Batley had a somewhat *laissez-faire* attitude to your account.'

Fleur, with difficulty, kept quiet. The woman was confusing Brian's understanding of the long-term planning involved in plant breeding, his support during a difficult period, with inactivity. But telling her so was unlikely to win her any Brownie points.

'The whole thing,' Delia Johnson went on, well into her stride now, 'reeks of…' she seemed to have difficulty locating exactly the right word '…cosiness.'

'On the contrary.' So much for keeping quiet. 'Brian knew how difficult things have been in the last few years. He took the long-term view, well aware of just what we've achieved in the past, knowing that given time, support, we'd come through again.'

'On what evidence? Your business is growing plants. How can your father do that if he can't leave the house?'

'I didn't say he can't leave the house,' she said protectively. 'And besides, we specialise in fuchsias, Ms Johnson, and, as I'm sure you know, they're grown under glass.'

She tried not to sound smug, but it was an unanswerable comeback.

'If that's the case, why have you taken charge of the business?'

Unanswerable, apparently, was not a concept Delia Johnson understood.

'Because it was my destiny from the moment I was born,' Fleur offered. 'And because I have a degree in horticultural management.'

'You need more than a degree, you need experience.'

There was just no stopping this woman, and it was true that Fleur hadn't anticipated having to take it all on quite so soon. The idea had been for her to work for other growers, widen her knowledge, as Matt had been doing. She'd been about to start working alongside him at one of the major growers— one of the advantages about the fact that their parents didn't speak to each other had been that neither family had realised that they were working for the same company—when her world had imploded.

But that was life for you. The first thing to go was the plan...

'I'm twenty-seven,' she said. Just. 'And I've been working in this business since I was old enough to pot a cutting.'

Too late she wondered if that would provoke an inquisition about the use of child labour, but Ms Johnson had enough sense not to take her literally. She had a more pressing row to hoe.

'So your father does what exactly?' she asked. She glanced at the file in front of her. 'He still draws a salary from the company.'

'My father is fully occupied in the breeding of new plant varieties. He rarely leaves his private boiler.'

'Boiler?'

'Glasshouse. They were originally heated by steam from coal-fired boilers and they were known as boilers. Ours have been in continuous use for six generations and the name seems to have stuck despite the fact that we no longer have to shovel coal to keep up the heat.' She tried a smile but, getting no encouragement from Delia Johnson, abandoned it. 'Heat, light, water…it's all electronically controlled these days.'

They had been amongst the first growers to install the new technology, borrowing deep, beating Hanovers to it by a whisker; at the time that had seemed like a coup, but the Hanovers had changed direction. All it meant now was that it was long past the time when it should have been ripped out and replaced.

'Six generations?'

'Seven with me. On that site, anyway. Bartholomew Gilbert and James Hanover formed a partnership to buy the land and build the glasshouses in 1829.'

'Really? I didn't know that the two companies had once been in partnership.'

'It was a very short-lived alliance. When James caught his pretty young wife *in flagrante* with Bart in one of the boilers, the land and the plant stock were divided, fences erected and the Gilberts and Hanovers have not spoken since.'

'Never?'

Never say never…

'But you live and work right next door to each other. How can you possibly sustain a grudge for that long?'

'I think "grudge" is putting it rather lightly. They fought over the division of the land, each believing the other had come off best. The same with the stock. Bart produced a new cultivar that year which James swore was his work.'

'I see.'

'The children took in the bad feeling with their mother's milk. The fact that they were in direct competition, vying for the position of premier fuchsia growers, did nothing to lessen the animosity. There were instances of sabotage, industrial espionage—'

'Excuse me?'

'Workers bribed to steal precious new cultivars. To introduce vine weevils into the stock.'

'Good grief.'

And, of course, what was forbidden was always going to tempt the reckless. Who was it who said that those who did not learn from history were doomed to repeat it?'

'Has anyone attempted to mediate, heal the rift?' asked Ms Johnson.

'Not with any success. On the last occasion half the village ended up in court on a charge of breaching the peace.'

Only the boundless optimism of youth had convinced her and Matt that they could finally reunite the families, heal a hundred and seventy years of discord with the power of their love.

Unfortunately, her mother and his father had been way ahead of them.

'I do see that to the outsider it must seem a bit like a cross between the plot of a Catherine Cookson saga and a James Bond movie,' Fleur said, rather fearing that, instead of involving the woman with company history, she'd just made things worse.

'Yes. Well, family feuds are no concern of mine. Your business account is another matter. Given the fact that you've been trading, in one way or another, for a hundred and seventy-five years, you've had more than enough time to get it right. The Hanovers, despite the distractions, appear to have managed their affairs somewhat more successfully.'

On safer ground, Fleur said, 'The Hanovers gave up plant production six years ago when Phillip Hanover died. They leave other people to take the risks these days.'

'Maybe you should consider following their example.'

'I doubt there's room for two gardening hypermarkets in Longbourne. Besides, if everyone did that, there would be no plants for Hanovers to sell. And fewer jobs to help support the local economy.'

Ms Johnson gave a shrug, apparently prepared to admit that she might have a point—albeit a very small one. Encouraged, Fleur went on, 'Any business that is at the mercy of weather and fashion is never going to be a smooth ride. In that we're no different from the High Street chain stores.'

'There are fashions in plants?'

'Television make-over programmes have raised the profile of gardening, but they do need a continuous supply of something new to offer the viewer. It takes the novel, the unexpected, to make an impact.' It was Fleur's turn to give a little shrug, implying that a woman with her finger on the pulse of business would know all about that. 'Unfortunately, breeding plants is a bit like steering one of those supertankers—it takes a long time before anything happens. It's just as well that plant breeders are a passionate bunch.'

'Sustaining a feud for the best part of two centuries would seem to require a certain amount of passion,' Ms Johnson agreed drily.

Refusing to rise to this, Fleur said, 'I had in mind the men and women who strive for years, generations, centuries to produce the impossible. The perfect black tulip, true blue rose, red daffodil.'

'Are you going to make my day and tell me you're planning to exhibit one of those at Chelsea this year?'

'No, but then, as you already know, we grow fuchsias.'

'So you do. And what is the Grail of the fuchsia grower?'

'A full double in buttercup-yellow.' She shrugged. 'A bit blowsy for the purists, but it would make the cover of all the gardening magazines.'

'Really. Wouldn't it be simpler, if you want bright yellow, to plant buttercups?'

'We're talking about the rare, Ms Johnson. Not garden weeds.'

Unperturbed, she responded, 'Is that what your father is spending his time working on?'

'He's been working on it all his life.'

'May I suggest that he'd be more productively occupied searching for a way to reduce your overdraft?' She sat back in her chair. 'My predecessor held you on a very loose rein, but I'm going to be frank with you, Miss Gilbert. I cannot allow the present situation to continue.'

Fleur's stomach clenched. 'The overdraft is secured on our land,' she said, praying that the internal wobbles hadn't migrated to her voice. 'The risk, surely, is all ours?'

'It's agricultural land and the equity is becoming perilously small, which is why I've instructed a surveyor to carry out a current valuation. He'll be getting in touch with you some time this week to arrange a convenient time.'

'And no doubt you'll be adding his fees to our overdraft?' Fleur did her best to stifle her outrage, but it was beyond disguising. 'That's no way to reduce it.'

'My duty is to protect the bank,' Delia Johnson said, getting to her feet, signalling that the meeting was at an end.

'We need two months,' Fleur said, not moving. She hadn't been given a chance to make her pitch. 'We need Chelsea to showcase our new varieties.'

'Isn't that a massive expense?'

'The RHS does not charge for space, but of course there are costs. Transport, accommodation, the catalogue. You'll find them itemised in the folder I've given you. It's a very small outlay in return for the publicity on the television, radio, in the print media. For the sales we'll make from the stand.'

'Right now the only plans I'm interested in concern the reduction of your overdraft.' She crossed to the door and opened it. 'I need something on my desk a week from today. When I've had time to look at it I'll come out to the nursery and talk to your father.'

Fleur considered standing her ground, insisting on making her pitch. Realising it would be to deaf ears, she saved her breath, picked up her briefcase and headed for the door. This was no longer a request for backing until May, it was a fight to stay in business.

CHAPTER TWO

SHE should have held out for the diamonds, Fleur thought as she climbed aboard the Land Rover. They'd have come in handy right now.

She reached up and took the tiny jewels from her ears that Matt had given her, cupping them in the palm of her hand. When he'd given them to her they'd seemed the most precious things in the world, but they were no more than pretty trinkets, worth as little as the till-death-us-do-part promise that went with them.

She tightened her hand around them, held them for a moment before dropping them in her pocket beside the letter from his mother.

They'd be in good company, she thought, reaching forward to turn the key in the ignition, before slumping back in the seat as the sting of tears caught her out.

She closed her eyes to trap them, refusing to let them fall. There wasn't a Hanover in the world worth a single one of her tears. If she needed reminding of that, she need look no further than the latest diatribe from Katherine Hanover.

She took out the crumpled envelope, determined to rip it in two, but as she grasped it, something, no more than a prickle of unease, stopped her.

Maybe it was the fact that it was addressed to her, maybe it was the wake-up call from the bank, but some basic instinct warned her not to ignore this letter. That somehow it was different. And pushing her thumb beneath the flap, she tore it open.

The note inside was short.

Fleur, she read.

She almost laughed at that. If there was one thing to admire about Katherine Hanover, it was her total lack of hypocrisy. No mushy, insincere 'Dear' for her. And the formality of 'Miss Gilbert' would have given her too much importance.

As she began to read, however, all inclination to smile left her.

As a matter of courtesy I'm writing to let you know that I will be instructing my solicitor to apply to the Family Court for a blood test in order to establish that I am the father of Thomas Gilbert. Should you choose to fight me, despite the fact that simple arithmetic would seem to make the outcome a foregone conclusion, you will be held responsible for all the costs involved.

Once paternity has been established, be assured that I will vigorously pursue a claim for custody of my son.

Matt

For a split second the name overrode every other emotion.

Matt?

Matt was home?

There was a moment of confused hope before reality brought her crashing back to earth.

The Family Court. Blood tests. Custody…

Then she was tearing at her scarf, clawing it from about her throat, gasping for breath as the contents of the letter, rather than its author, struck home, driving the air from her body. The coldness of the words chilled her to the bone.

Matt had written this? Her Matt had applied these foul words to paper?

She stared at the letter, lying where it had fallen at her feet, scarcely able, even now, to believe him capable of such cruelty.

He hadn't even troubled himself to pick up a pen. He'd typed it, sitting in front of a PC as he'd put those knife-edged words together before sending it, with the impersonal click of a mouse, to print. Only his name had been written in the bold cursive that she'd once known as well as her own hand.

Just the one word. *Matt.*

None of the words, full of love, that he'd once used to close his notes to her. No little drawings of flowers. No kisses.

Only the words *Hanovers—Everything For Your Garden,* embossed in blue and gold on the pale grey paper, to mock her.

He hadn't even bothered to use personal notepaper, but had written to her on the company letterhead.

Then what?

Had he stuffed it into an envelope before, too impatient to wait for the mail to take its time about delivering his bombshell, he'd walked the hundred yards from his front gate to hers, to push it through her letterbox?

Had he been that close and she hadn't felt his presence? Hadn't known that he was just feet away?

She covered her mouth with her hand, as if to hold in the pain.

Would he have taken the risk of being seen by his mother? Did she know?

Her head began to swim at the thought.

No.

She clutched at the steering wheel, as if to a lifeline, forcing herself to swallow down the rising tide of panic.

No.

If Katherine Hanover had even suspected that Tom was her grandson there would have been no warning. The first she'd have known about it would have been a letter from the woman's lawyer. There had been enough of those in the last few years.

A sagging fence. The branch of a tree daring to intrude over Hanover land. The slightest excuse to make their lives difficult had brought the threat of the law down on them.

No. She knew nothing about this.

But the cold reference to blood tests, the Family Court, costs, that was pure Hanover. This man whom she'd loved at first sight, had deceived her parents to meet, had married in secret, who had declared he would love her until death, had written this unfeeling note with as little compassion as if she were a bug, something to be squashed between his fingers.

And suddenly it was anger, rather than fear, surging through her veins.

How dared he turn up now, out of the blue, after all these years and demand his *rights?* He had no rights. Not morally, anyway.

Not that the morality of the case would matter a damn when it came to the law. She knew that his lawyers would obtain a court order if she refused to allow the blood test.

At least he hadn't added insult to injury by suggesting the result was in doubt.

But that was small comfort. Once the blood test proved his claim, the Family Court would probably decide that she was the one at fault for depriving a man of his son and he would be occupying the moral high ground.

But that wasn't how it had been.

He was the one who'd left.

She hadn't had that luxury. She hadn't been able to pack her bags, leave the country, start a new life, not with her mother in intensive care, her father in the throes of a breakdown.

There had been no way to hide the fact that she was expecting a baby from the speculative stares of the village gossips. She'd had to stay and face down the sudden silences whenever she'd gone into the village shop. As if she didn't know exactly what they'd been saying. That she was no better than her mother.

Even the women who took their wages every week from her hand, who'd known her all her life, had thrilled themselves with whispers that the only reason she wouldn't tell the father's name was because she couldn't. That she didn't know.

She knew. That was the reason she'd kept silent.

There had only ever been one man in her life and she had both dreamed of and dreaded this moment.

Had dreamed of Matt bursting into the house, gathering them both up in his arms and begging her to forgive him.

Had dreaded having to admit what she'd done to her father. The lies, the deceit.

Exactly like her mother.

And, like an asthmatic grabbing for an inhaler, she flung open the Land Rover door to suck the chill air deep into her lungs.

An angry blast from a passing motorist who'd been forced to swerve out of the way brought her back to her senses. She banged the door shut and sat there for a moment, trying to block out the panic, the pain. She had no right to think of herself, indulge in self-pity, misery, waste energy raging against fate.

Only Tom mattered. His world, until now, had consisted of her, his grandfather, his life in the village. All that was about to change and she was going to have to make what was about to happen as simple, as straightforward, as painless for him as she could.

She didn't have the luxury of time to formulate a strategy. She had to react to the situation as it had been presented to her and her first task was to put a stop to the blood test. Now.

She picked up the letter, dug out her mobile phone and, without stopping to think about what she was going to say, punched in the number. It rang only once before a familiar voice said, 'Matthew Hanover.'

She nearly dropped the phone. She'd been prepared for a receptionist, a secretary, even for Katherine Hanover to answer the telephone, although if it had been Katherine she'd have hung up.

And she discovered that his voice, even now, went straight to her heart's core, leaving her feeling bone weak.

After a moment she lifted the phone back to her ear. There was no prompt, no puzzled 'Hello.' He'd been waiting for her to ring. Knew it was her. Let the cruel silence stretch on for what seemed like minutes as he waited for her to speak, as she tried to find some word to break the silence.

How are you? What have you been doing for the last six years? I missed you...

In her dreams words hadn't been necessary, but this wasn't a dream, it was a nightmare.

'I—I received your letter,' she said finally. Then, quickly, before she fell apart, 'There's no need for a blood test. I don't want Tom to go through that.'

'I'm not particularly interested in what you want, Fleur,' he replied, like her ignoring the niceties and going straight to the heart of the thing. 'I just want the truth.'

Straight to the point, his mother's son.

'You know the truth.'

'Maybe I do, but I have a right to have it confirmed. Apparently the gossip in the village is that you don't know who Tom's father is.'

'You know better than to listen to gossip.' Then, because this wasn't about her, 'He's so little, Matt. He won't understand. I don't want him to be frightened.'

'You should have thought of that before. You've had it your way for five years. Now I'm dictating the terms.'

'Please…' She heard herself begging and didn't care. 'I'll do anything.'

There was another seemingly endless silence before he said, very softly, 'Anything?'

It was just as well that Matt gave her no chance to confirm or deny it.

'Very well. Meet me tonight at the barn,' he said briskly, as businesslike as if he were making an appointment to clear up some unfinished business—and maybe he did see it that way. 'We can discuss exactly what "anything" means then.'

The barn? She covered her mouth with her hand, shutting in the cry of pain. Had he chosen the location, their special place, deliberately to hurt her?

But then, where else would they meet? In the village pub? That would certainly give the gossips a field day. The alternative was driving halfway across the county to find somewhere where there was no risk of them being recognised. If he'd been making enquiries about them, he must know that she didn't have the time for that.

She breathed in and out once, very slowly, then said, 'I won't be able to get out until late.'

'Nothing has changed, then.' There was the faintest sound, a sigh of resignation perhaps. 'Come when you can. I'll wait.'

Matt pressed the disconnect button.

Please...

If he closed his eyes he could still see her, eighteen years old, lying back on a bed of straw in the old hayloft, her green eyes soft, her mouth warm and inviting. *'Please...'*

Even now, after all that had happened, he still responded like a horny teenager to the sound of her voice. Had to work to remember his anger.

'Did I hear the phone?'

His mother paused in the doorway as if careful of invading his space, apparently unaware that checking up on his phone calls was even more intrusive.

'Yes,' he said and, taking that as an invitation, she joined him, setting her bag down on what she was already referring to as 'his' desk, and he glanced up. 'I've been offered a cottage in Upper Haughton,' he said. True enough. But not the answer to her question. Nothing, it seemed, had changed.

He and Fleur were both still locked in by nearly two centuries of hatred. They were both still lying to their parents, creeping out to meet in secret. But, while playing Romeo and Juliet had had a certain illicit appeal when they'd been too young to recognise the dangers, he'd had his fill of subterfuge.

'You're not staying here?' she asked, trying hard to disguise her disappointment.

'I've arranged to pick up the keys from the owner this evening.'

'Renting a cottage in Upper Haughton will cost a pretty penny.'

'It's just as well I've inherited your business acumen, then.'

The compliment brought a smile to her face, as he'd known it would. But she wasn't happy and, unable to stop herself, she said, 'Why on earth waste good money, when there's all the room you need here? You've been away for so long. I'd like the chance to spend some time with you. Cosset you a little.'

Yes, well, he'd been angry with her too, and cruel, as only the young, with time on their side, can be. He regretted that, but not enough to live under the same roof as her. But he reached out, briefly touching her arm, to soften the rejection as he said, 'It isn't far.' Just far enough to avoid prying eyes. 'If I decide to stay, I'll look around for somewhere permanent to buy.'

'Of course,' she agreed, immediately retreating, as if walking on eggs. 'I still can't quite think of you as…well, an adult. Clearly the last thing a grown man of means wants is to live at home with his mother.' Then, 'What about the office?' She did a good job of keeping the need, the fear that he'd leave again, from her voice as she gestured around her at the office she'd placed at his disposal. 'Will this do you for the moment, or will you need more room?' she asked, quickly recovering and giving him the opportunity for a graceful exit. Demonstrating that, no matter how desperate she was to cling to him, she wasn't going to make a fool of herself.

He hadn't discussed his plans with her, but only because he didn't yet know what they were. He could work from the cottage, but an office at Hanovers gave him an excuse to come into the village whenever he wanted, so he said, 'The use of a spare desk is welcome until I decide what I'm going to do.'

'For as long as you like.'

'No, for as long as you don't try to drag me into your war with the Gilberts.' If it hadn't been for that nonsense…

'I'm not at war with them, Matt,' she said, and laughed as if the very idea were ridiculous. 'I'm just doing my best to make a living.'

'And your best is very good indeed,' he said, not convinced by her swift denial but, having made his point, happy to change the subject. He got up, crossing to the window. 'You've made an extraordinary success of this. Dad wouldn't recognise the place.'

'No.' There was just a hint of self-satisfaction in her voice, Matt thought, turning to look at her. His father wouldn't have recognised her, either.

She'd been one of those dull, practically invisible women, never getting involved in the business. Always ready to give a helping hand at village functions, but never, like some mothers—like Fleur's mother—drawing attention to herself with her clothes or her make-up, something for which he'd been deeply grateful as a boy. Seeing her now, every inch the stylish and successful businesswoman, he wondered about that. About how unhappy she must have been.

'What made you change your mind about selling up, moving away?' he asked, keeping his own voice even, emotionless.

'Time, maybe. I spent the best part of a year trying to sell it, hating every minute that I was forced to stay here. Unfortunately, the only people who showed an interest were housing developers but, much as I'd have enjoyed seeing a rash of nasty little houses on Hanover land, I couldn't get planning permission.'

He didn't bother to remind her that he'd pleaded with her to let him run the place for her. That she could have left, settled in comfort wherever she liked on the pension his father had provided. He was sure she'd thought about it many times during the last six years.

'You must have really hated him.'

'I wasn't thinking straight at the time. If I had been, I would have realised that I wasn't the only person hurting.'

It was as near to an apology as he was going to get, he thought and shrugged. 'You did me a favour. Prised me out of a rut I'd been stuck in since I was old enough to know that my life was all laid out for me.'

She glanced at him, a frown creasing her forehead, and for a moment he suspected she hadn't been thinking about him at all. Then she smiled and said, 'That's generous of you.' She turned back to the window. 'The truth is that I was pretty much at rock bottom when two men turned up full of plans for turning the place into a low-cost pile-'em-high-and-sell-'em-cheap garden centre. They were talking about finance, turnover, suppliers, as if I wasn't there and I realised that I'd been invisible for most of my life.'

This was so close to what he'd just been thinking that Matt felt more than a touch uncomfortable. 'So,' he said, 'you got your own back on them by nicking all their ideas?'

'Far from it. Their ideas were rubbish. They were missing the whole point. This business isn't just about dumping everything in a warehouse and selling the basics at the cheapest price. You have to sell gardening, the garden, as you would an expensive kitchen or good furniture. It's got to be desirable, a lifestyle.' And finally she smiled. 'You've got to appeal to the women.'

'Did you tell them that?'

'I thought about it.' She shrugged. 'They'd have just looked at me in that puzzled way that men do and then carry on as if I hadn't spoken, but after they'd gone I couldn't stop thinking about it.'

'You had no trouble with planning permission? Change of use?'

'I'd learned my lesson. I had my hair cut, bought a decent suit, turned myself into someone men would take seriously. I put it to the planners that I simply wanted to change the emphasis from growing to selling. Then I went to the bank and showed them my figures, my business plan.'

'There were no objections from the neighbours?' he asked, looking across at the solid stone house, the roofs of the Gilbert glasshouses just visible above the fence. 'Not even from Seth Gilbert?'

'Not even from him. Maybe he felt sorry for me.'

'His mistake.'

'Yes,' she said. Then, almost to herself, 'Not his first.'

Even on a Monday morning the car park was busy with people loading trays of plants, bags of compost, all the attractive garden hardware his mother stocked. 'You could do with more space,' he said.

'I'll have all the space I need soon,' she said, joining him at the window. 'You could have the Gilbert house if you wait a few months. It'll need a lot of work, but it'll make a lovely family home.'

'It will?' He frowned. 'You've been inside? When?'

She started as if caught out in something illicit. 'Oh, not in decades,' she said. 'But Seth's mother used to throw wonderful parties.' She flapped her hand across her face as if brushing away a memory that clung like a cobweb.

'And you were invited to these parties?' he persisted.

'I wasn't always a Hanover.' Then she arranged her face into a smile and said, 'Think about the house. It's time you settled down, thought about getting married. Is there anyone?' She didn't wait for his answer, but said, 'I'm getting broody for grandchildren.'

He'd assumed that the newspaper cutting had been sent by

his mother, that she'd seen the photograph and, spotting some resemblance to him as a child, the kind of thing that only she would notice, she'd suspected the truth, had used it as a lure to bring him home. Nothing in her manner suggested it, however, and her face gave nothing away. But then, it occurred to him, it never had. She'd been not so much dull as blank.

'I'd rather have the barn,' he replied.

'The barn?'

'I've always thought it would make a lovely home. I've seen some stunning conversions.'

She turned away abruptly. 'Sorry, Matt, but I've already got the plans drawn up to turn that into a restaurant.'

'A restaurant?'

'Customers expect more than a cup of coffee and a bun at garden centres these days,' she said and opened a cabinet, using the desk to lay out a bundle of drawings, an architect's sketch of how it would look.

'Seth Gilbert's agreed to sell?' he asked, surprised. His agent hadn't reported that.

'I've put in a fair offer for the whole site, including the barn and house. I'm still waiting for him to come to his senses and accept.'

Satisfied, he said, 'Maybe he doesn't consider your offer as fair as you do.'

'I'm not a charity,' she replied, 'but if he chooses to go bankrupt then there's nothing I can do about it.'

'Is that inevitable?' he asked, as if he didn't already know to the last penny how much Seth Gilbert owed to the bank. He hadn't wasted the weeks he'd been forced to delay in Hungary. He'd put the time to good use, acquiring documents, information, legal advice, everything he needed to ensure he got exactly what he wanted.

And it was working.

He'd been home less than twenty-four hours and already Fleur had picked up the telephone and called him. And, in her panic, had told him everything he needed to know.

She'd do anything…

He closed his hand to stop it from shaking and made an effort to tune back in to what his mother was saying.

'…sooner rather than later. You need to have something no one else has, or be able to work on a much bigger scale these days. No matter. I'll sit him out and buy from the bank when he goes under.'

'But in the meantime you've somehow managed to obtain a set of drawings of the barn.'

She shrugged. 'A local builder submitted plans to the local council for converting it into holiday cottages. He was happy to sell them to me when he was turned down.'

'I'll bet. So that's Plan A. What's Plan B?'

'Plan B?'

'The fallback plan. I can see that the semi-rural location has a certain charm, but have you considered that you might do a great deal better if you moved the whole operation to the business park?'

'I don't want to move. And to have a fallback plan suggests that I'm prepared to lose.'

So much for her denial that she was at war.

'Well?' Her father glanced up from the standard fuchsia he was working on as Fleur placed a cup of tea beside him on the staging.

'What?'

'What did this new woman at the bank have to say for herself?'

'Oh…'

The letter, her brief conversation with Matt, an insidious fear that once Katherine Hanover was involved she'd use her money, influence, the power base she'd built up in the community to snatch her son away from her, had driven everything else from her mind.

She couldn't even remember the journey home.

'I, um, left the Chelsea stuff with her to look at in detail.'

'You didn't discuss it with her?'

Concentrate, concentrate…

'She's more concerned about the overdraft. She wants to talk again next week. To both of us.' Then, because there was no way to shield him from reality, 'After we've come up with a plan to reduce it.'

'Tell her she'll have to wait until the third week in May,' he said, returning to the task in hand, grooming the plant with the tip of a razor-sharp knife before, satisfied, he offered the pot to her for her to look at. 'Then she'll see for herself.'

'Will she?' The label bore only a number and a date. 'Is this it?'

'It'll be a show-stopper,' he said. 'A Gold Medal certainty.'

'Always assuming that we're still in business come the end of May.'

Always assuming her father wasn't living in cloud-cuckoo-land.

'There'll be people who'll turn their noses up at it, no doubt,' he said.

'The ones who think that if you want buttercup-yellow you should grow buttercups?' she said, thinking of the bank manager. 'We'd still be picking wild grasses to make flour for bread if they had their way.'

'It's going to be primrose, not buttercup.' He rubbed at

one of his eyes, blinked as if to clear his vision. 'Give me another year…'

'We can't wait another year.' She offered him back the plant but, as he reached for it, he pulled back, shook his hand, flexing it.

'Are you all right, Dad?'

'I'm fine,' he said a touch irritably. 'Don't fuss, just put that on the bench.'

She watched him for a moment, concerned that he was overdoing it, but after a moment he reached for another plant and carried on working, leaving her to ponder the more urgent question of finances.

The fact of the matter was that they needed a true yellow to make the breakthrough. Primrose was a lot closer to cream. And cream wouldn't do.

If he was just fooling himself…

Pushing the uncertainties to the back of her mind she said, 'Ms Johnson said she would come out to the nursery and have a look around next week.' She looked along the ranks of fuchsias that had been planted at weekly intervals, staggering the peak of flowering over a three-week period in order to guarantee perfection for a single week in May. Would she be impressed? Or simply see a glasshouse packed with plants that were all outlay, no income? 'I'm going to have to tell her what we've got.'

'You'll do no such thing,' he declared roundly.

The vehemence of his reply took her by surprise. 'Dad, I don't think you understand—'

'I understand perfectly. Do you want to see someone else inviting the press to look at their stunning breakthrough a week before Chelsea? Years of work with someone else's name on it?' He seemed a little—*hectic,* she thought as he gestured at the bench in front of them. Too keyed-up. It wasn't good for his blood pressure. 'We can't afford the kind of security that would be needed if so much as a hint gets out that I've made the breakthrough.' Then, without warning, his face creased in a wicked grin that reminded her of the way he used to be. 'That's one of the advantages of everyone thinking you're past it, my girl. You can stop worrying about who's going to steal your new cultivars.'

She laughed to cover her sigh. Security. Just one more thing to worry about. 'At least this is one thing we've got that Katherine Hanover isn't interested in.'

'Katherine Hanover would kill to have her name instead of ours on this.'

She frowned. 'Why? No one would believe she'd bred it.'

'Possession is nine-tenths of the law in this game, but this isn't just about pride, or about putting the Gilbert name back at the forefront of plant breeding. This is to secure Tom's future.'

'I don't think you understand, Dad. Ms Johnson needs something to justify supporting us.'

'Exactly. She'll tell her head office, some bright spark there will ask around to see if she knows what the devil she's talking about and once she's done that it won't be a secret any more.'

'But—'

'No buts.'

'Won't the fact that we're making the effort to go to Chelsea this year, after such a long break, have already aroused some speculation?'

'If anyone asks, we're relaunching Gilberts, and if they snigger, think I'm fooling myself, you let them.'

That was so close to what she had been thinking that she almost cringed with guilt, but facts had to be faced.

A major grower would have used the latest cell propagation technology to produce thousands of plants in the first year. Because of her father's secrecy they'd had no choice but to propagate the old-fashioned way. Amongst the hundreds of plants being prepared for the show, only a small proportion were cuttings from the precious plant her father claimed to have produced the previous year.

If only he'd shown her, allowed her to photograph the blooms so that they had something to show for all his work, but he hadn't said a word until the RHS had offered them space at Chelsea and she'd demanded to know what on earth he thought he was going to put in it.

It was such a very fragile thing, a plant. A single mishap could wipe them all out, at least for this year, and next year would be too late.

'Oh, well,' she said, doing her best to look cheerful, 'we'll be packing the second crop of plugs for despatch next week. At least we'll look industrious if Ms Johnson does decide to come and take a look around.'

'Just keep her out of here,' he said, his attention already back on his work.

'Dad?' She swallowed. 'I'll have to slip out later this evening for an hour or so. I promised I'd give Sarah Carter a hand with the arrangements for the village Easter egg hunt next week.'

The lie stuck in her throat. Had her mother made excuses like that to cover her illicit meetings with Phillip Hanover? Afterwards, she'd tried to remember, but she'd been too busy inventing her own reasons to escape the house to take much notice what her mother was doing—after all, parents weren't expected to have a life. They certainly weren't supposed to be indulging in the same thrillingly illicit passion that had become the centre of her own secret world.

Feeling slightly sick, she said, 'Can you keep an eye on Tom for me?'

'I won't be going anywhere,' he said, not looking up from what he was doing.

What did you wear to meet a man you'd once thought the world well lost for? A man who, when it had come to making a stand, a choice, hadn't loved her enough?

A man you wanted to impress, even while you wanted him to see that you didn't care a hoot for his opinion?

Making an effort for the bank manager had been child's play in comparison. A tidy suit, shoes brightly polished, neat hair.

A no-brainer.

But that had been business.

What did you wear when you were going to be begging a man not to destroy the one infinitely precious part of your life to have emerged from the wreckage? All that remained of the bright future they had planned together, the single joy that gave a point to getting out of bed each morning.

In the event, it was the weather—the damp chill rain of a spring slow to get started—and her destination, an ancient barn at the end of a muddy, little-used footpath, which decided the matter for her, saving her from any pathetic attempt to look alluring. To turn his head. Remind him that he'd loved her once.

As if she could.

Six hard years had knocked the bloom from her appearance. Warm trousers, sturdy ankle boots, an old soft shirt worn under a roomy sweater would do the job. And the clothes dictated the rest of her appearance. The minimum of make-up, her hair tied back in a plait. That was who she was now. A young village matron, more concerned with school, church, keeping her business ticking over, her son's welfare, than her own appearance.

She tied the laces in her boots and straightened her back, doing her best to ignore the ache. She'd spent the afternoon on her knees fixing the pump that drove the mist sprays. Her back hurt, her fingers were sore and bruised where she'd knocked them against unforgiving metal.

'I'm off, Dad,' she called from the hall as she shrugged into a waxed jacket, soft and dull from wear. 'Tom's flat out. He shouldn't bother you.'

'He's no bother.'

On an impulse she went back, put her hand on his shoulder and kissed his forehead.

He didn't look up from the horticultural journal he was reading. He just said, 'You never told me what Katherine Hanover wanted.'

'What?' Caught off balance, she floundered, finally managing to stammer out, 'N-nothing. Everything. The usual.'

'Nothing to worry about, then.'

He knew, she thought. He knew she was lying. And, without any warning, a picture of her mother slipped into her head—her slim white hand on his shoulder, the diamonds in her engagement ring sparkling in the lamplight, the slide of her thick fair hair as she bent to place a Judas kiss on her husband's forehead even as she'd spewed out some lie before going to meet her lover.

'Dad… About the letter…'

He covered her hand with his own. 'It'll keep, Fleur. You don't want to be late.' Then, glancing up, 'Tell Sarah to keep one for me.'

'What?'

'An Easter egg. Just a little one.'

'Oh. Yes.' And she laughed, more with relief than amusement, realising that, after all, it was just her guilty conscience driving her imagination. It was so long since she'd done this. Pretending that she'd needed to borrow a book for homework, or lend a CD to a friend, setting out in the direction of the village before doubling back in the dark along the footpath to the old barn. 'I'll tell her.'

She paused for a moment as she stepped through the back door.

'Basket, Cora,' she said as, tail wagging hopefully, the dog whimpered hopefully from the step. 'Dad will take you out later.'

She wished she were just taking the dog for a walk.

Once her heart would have been pounding with a mixture of guilt, elation, joy at the prospect of meeting Matt.

It was pounding hard enough as she walked around the house but this time the guilt was not leavened with excitement. This time there was only desperate fear as her footsteps rang first on the stone path, then crunched over the gravel before, finally, she reached the quieter surface of the lane, every step a journey into the past.

She knew every sound, instinctively remembered the exact number of steps before she was out of sight of the house.

Once she'd been a girl rushing to meet her lover and only that moment, that meeting was important. The future was something to worry about when it happened.

It just had.

CHAPTER THREE

MATT didn't remember being this impatient when they were young. Maybe it was the added element of uncertainty that made him so restless now. Of course back then he'd never doubted that Fleur would come. Even if she'd had to wait until everyone was in bed and climb out over the scullery roof to avoid the burglar alarm, she'd always made it, sooner or later.

Now…

He glanced at his watch for the third time in five minutes. It was still a couple of minutes short of nine and she'd warned him that she might be late but, sick of pacing the barn floor, he went outside, straining for the giveaway sounds of her approach along the footpath. Hoping to catch the glimmer of a hooded torch beam…

He came close to smiling, then.

Of course he'd been impatient.

How could he have forgotten the way he'd rushed to meet her as soon as he'd spotted her light, unable to wait another second for that first kiss? To just hold her. Both of them breathless, but not from running.

He resumed his pacing in front of the barn, heedless of the cold and damp seeping into his limbs. His memory, now it had been jogged, spared him nothing of the urgency of the longing that had driven him then, whether he'd seen her the night before, or it had been the seemingly endless weeks apart while he was away at university. The even longer separations once she was at college and he was working at the other end of the country, gaining experience before he joined his father at Hanovers.

Once she'd graduated he'd persuaded her, against her better judgement, to marry him before confronting their parents with a *fait accompli,* certain that once they were so indivisibly joined no one could ever drive a wedge between them.

How naïve he'd been to think he could fly in the face of history.

The ties of blood had been more powerful than any emotion she'd ever felt for him. Even pregnant with his child, she'd chosen to outface the village gossips rather than admit the truth to her father: that she'd lain with a Hanover.

Well, he was using that family feeling against her now, counting on her to play for time. But she'd had the entire afternoon to recover from her first panicked reaction and while she was, no doubt, still determined to protect her father from the shock, there had been nothing to prevent her, older, wiser, from using the afternoon to seek legal advice. Not that it would help her in the long run.

Nothing she could do would keep him from his son, but a wise lawyer would surely have warned her against meeting him on her own, persuaded her to let him arrange something controllable, with an adviser or counsellor present to protect everyone's interests.

Of course she might just have grabbed Tom and run with him. She wouldn't leave her father for him, but for her child...

On that bitter thought he turned and saw a tiny beam of light swinging erratically as someone climbed the stile.

* * *

Fleur would have known where to stop even without the tiny beam of the light on her keyring searching out the gap in the overgrown hedge.

Her feet still remembered the number of steps. Her hand reached for the top bar of the stile guarding the footpath that skirted the Gilbert land, and connected with it as confidently as if it had been broad daylight. She stepped up, over the bar and down on to the far side as smoothly if she'd done it every day for the last six years, instead of avoiding it like the plague.

She'd thought the lane dark, but that had been an illusion, she discovered. The footpath was lower, tucked beneath a centuries-old hedge that blocked the light pollution from the main road bypassing the village and, as she stepped into its shadow, she discovered a thicker, blacker darkness that her light barely penetrated.

Had it always been like that? Or had the hedge, neglected like so many other things as she'd struggled to keep down running costs, just become overgrown?

Maybe, back then, racing towards the warmth of Matt's arms, she'd been so fired up with love that she'd made her own light.

Older, not much wiser but certainly more conscious of the dangers, she made slower progress now, one arm curved protectively in front of her face to avoid walking into a stem of bramble as she almost felt her way along the path. Telling herself, as she stumbled into a pothole and found a puddle deep enough to spill over the top of her boot and soak her sock, that she shouldn't be doing this.

But what was the alternative?

Half a dozen times that afternoon she'd reached for the phone, knowing that the sensible thing would be to call the family solicitor and get some advice. No need to mention names. Just say that Tom's father had turned up out of the blue and was demanding access…

But each time she'd stopped herself. Once the lawyers were involved there would be no chance of persuading Matt to be reasonable. To listen to her. To try to understand.

It was a forlorn hope. In his shoes she'd be feeling anything but reasonable and an involuntary sound, something between a sigh and a moan, escaped her lips. Regret, mostly. But maybe edged with just a touch of fear.

Matt had been the gentlest of boys, of men, but he must have changed in six years and, even if he hadn't, he was clearly very angry with her. She didn't blame him for that, but maybe this wasn't such a great idea…

Even as she hesitated, uncertain whether to go on or turn back, the crack of a twig warned her that she was not alone in the darkness. Her scream, pure reflex, a primal response to the unseen danger rather than the result of genuine fear, was cut off by a cold hand clamped over her face, while any possibility of retreat was blocked by an arm that locked around her waist, holding her fast.

'For heaven's sake, Fleur! Do you want the entire village to know our business?'

Matt. She'd known it even before he spoke. How could she not know? She had once been as familiar with his scent as her own. She knew the shape of his body, how it fitted so perfectly against hers, knew exactly how far back to tilt her head as she looked up into his face, even now, when it was too dark to make out his features. He had been the only man in her life and at his touch every one of her senses lit up like a New Year's Eve fireworks display. For one long moment all she wanted was to lean into him, surrender, let him have whatever he wanted, if only he'd go on holding her. Never let go of her again.

But while one arm was around her, steadying her, stopping her from falling, the other, warmer now, was still clamped over her mouth, keeping a safe distance between them, and there was nothing to do but shake her head, just once, so that he'd know she wasn't about to have hysterics. Reassured, he instantly backed off, taking away his hand so that the cold rushed back against her warmed skin, leaving her feeling bereft, alone, and for a moment she reconsidered the hysterics.

Rejecting anything so unutterably feeble, she declared, 'Idiot! You scared the wits out of me.'

'You were already scared.' And, grasping her wrist, he lifted the hand clutching the ridiculous little light she'd thought would be sufficient to keep her from pitching headlong into trouble, holding it up in front of her face. 'What *is* this?'

'A p-perfectly good light.' Then, because that was clearly anything but the case, 'Usually. I think the b-battery must be going.'

'And you have the nerve to call me an idiot?'

All day she'd been wondering what their first words would be after so long. As hard as their last? The tone of Matt's letter suggested as much. And the phone call had confirmed it. But deep down she'd been cherishing an obviously forlorn hope that when they saw one another it would be different. Fooling herself that, perhaps unconsciously he'd picked the barn for their meeting not, as she'd first thought, to hurt her, but because it was where they'd been happiest...

But not even her over-active imagination had stretched to this.

'It's nice to see you, too,' she said.

'You could have broken your ankle.'

He sounded exasperated rather than heartbroken at the prospect and she responded with what she hoped was a careless shrug and muttered, 'More likely my neck. Not that you'd have cared.'

'Of course I'd have cared,' he said, grasping her wrist even more firmly, as if afraid that even now she might bolt. 'I was saving the pleasure of wringing it for myself.'

He didn't wait to hear her response, which was just as well, since she was speechless, but turned and set off sure-footedly, despite the dark, in the direction of the barn.

She should have turned back when she had the chance, she thought—not that she took his threat seriously—but the firm grip of his fingers suggested she was fooling herself if she thought that, having got her here, he was about to let her escape.

What would have been the point, anyway, unless she'd been prepared to take Tom and run away, spend the rest of her life in hiding? She hadn't been able to abandon her father six years ago when Matt had gone all Biblical on her, turning up on her doorstep, bags packed, insisting she drop everything and go with him, leave everything she knew. A dying mother. Her father on the brink of a breakdown.

She certainly couldn't do it now, when everything depended on her.

Whatever he planned, she had no way of escaping it. He was calling all the shots and he knew it.

He pushed open the barn door just wide enough for them to squeeze through, releasing her the minute she was inside as if he couldn't bear to touch her, shutting it behind them to stop the light from escaping. The sound of the latch dropping into place had none of the comfort of those lost years, when being shut in here with him was about as perfect as life got.

It sounded doom-laden.

Like her mouth, her wrist felt cold without the warmth of

his touch and she shivered, covering the place with her own hand as if to hold on to something precious. At least it was dry inside and a gas lamp, hissing softly, threw a warm circle of light that encompassed the old sofa on which they'd once planned what they were going to do with their lives once they'd reunited their warring families, reunited Gilbert and Hanover. It created an illusion of cosy intimacy.

'It all looks exactly the same,' she said, looking at the furniture rather than face this cold stranger who sounded like Matt, but was nothing like the boy, the man, she'd fallen so desperately in love with.

'The lamp is new. The old one was rusted through.'

'Oh. You checked. I never thought…'

'I imagine you had other things on your mind. Where are you supposed to be tonight?'

Ah, well, then. Some things never changed.

He'd always asked her the same question back when they were young and, for just a moment, she thought that it was, after all, going to be okay and finally turned to face him, half expecting him to laugh or, cursing the fates that had separated them, pull her into his arms, tell her that he was sorry. That he'd been a fool. That he was home now and everything would be all right. That he'd never leave her again.

He didn't move; he just stood there with his hands pushed into the pockets of a long, dark cashmere overcoat, looking just the same, but somehow completely different. Older. That was it. Well, they were. A lifetime older in the six years since they'd last stood face to face and discovered that love was not enough.

But while she'd seen time do its worst to the face that stared back out at her from the mirror every morning, on him it looked good. The few unexpected threads of silver hair at his temples, the fine lines fanning from his eyes, carved into his cheeks, did no more than add character. Even as a boy glimpsed from her bedroom window—not just four impossibly distant years older but with the added glamour of the forbidden—he'd been a head turner.

Now that early promise had matured into the prime of manhood.

Undoubtedly successful—his clothes, everything about him breathed quality—he'd acquired assurance, the arrogance of a man who knew what he wanted and refused to take no for an answer. Perhaps he hadn't changed so much, after all, she thought, remembering the way he'd crushed all her doubts about their marriage, convinced her that it was the obvious thing, the only thing to do.

In her imagination he'd been in a kind of stasis, always hers, faithful to vows they should never have made, but this wasn't the Matt Hanover she'd married. He'd changed out of all recognition from the image of him that she'd held in her head for the last six years, even as her own reflection had aged in the mirror. He was a man, with a man's needs, and she had no doubt that he'd turned heads—as he'd turned hers—all the way to the top.

She turned away, struggling to hold down the sickly green feeling of jealousy that all but overwhelmed her. He was right not to offer hollow reassurance. How could anything be all right ever again?

Faced with the bitter reality, she stumbled to the sofa and sat down before the trembling in her legs betrayed her.

Matt thought she was going to fall and, despite his determination to make no move towards her, he reached out to steady her before he could stop himself.

She didn't notice and by the time she was safely on the sofa he had his hand back under control. This wasn't how it was supposed to be. He wasn't supposed to care. It had seemed so much simpler as he'd watched her from his bedroom window that morning—dressed for business, totally in control of her life. Even the green-eyed monster eating away at him, telling him that a woman like Fleur would not have waited, would have found someone else—had indeed found someone else—had seemed like a friend.

Tonight she'd left off the make-up, hadn't done more than the minimum with her hair, and she had to be wearing clothes she kept for working in the glasshouses. Damn it, he'd expected her to at least make an effort!

'Well?' he prompted harshly, fighting the temptation to soften. 'I don't imagine you told your father you were coming out to meet me.'

'No, I didn't do that.' She gave an awkward little shrug, as if ashamed at still having to make an excuse to meet him. Her problem, not his. 'I'm supposed to be meeting someone.'

'Anyone I know?'

She looked at him, as if about to tell him to mind his own business, then, 'Do you remember Sarah Duncan?'

'Bouncy girl? Mad about horses?'

'That's her. She married Sam Carter. We're organising the Easter egg hunt this year.'

'And you're supposed to be meeting her?' Well, they were old friends. She'd provided cover for them in the past; no doubt she was still doing it.

'I can't stay long, Matt.'

'What I have to say won't take long,' he assured her. Then she looked up at him, and he discovered that her green eyes needed no help to bewitch him. That no matter what she'd done, how much he despised her, it still only took a look to touch something deep at the very core of his heart. His soul.

This was a mistake.

He'd thought himself immune, numb to feeling. He'd wanted her to look him in the eyes and see what she'd done to him, acknowledge his pain.

He should have left it to the lawyers, kept his distance…

'What excuse did you make?' she asked.

Excuse? He wanted to tell her that these days Matt Hanover was his own man, that he hadn't had to explain his actions to anyone in a long time. Tell her that it was time she got a grip on her life, too.

Until twenty-four hours ago, it would have been true, but coming home was like stepping back in time. Everything was just as it had always been. Deep down nothing had changed.

His mother, her father, were both victims; they should have been weeping on one another's shoulders, not at each other's throats. Instead it was as if what had happened had spread the poison, affecting everyone it touched. Even those who'd been foolish enough to think themselves immune.

'I went to pick up the keys to a cottage before I came here. I imagine my mother thinks I'm spending the evening going through the inventory.' Not an excuse as such, but it was a fine line between telling a lie and not telling the truth.

'You're not going to be living at home?' Fleur asked, clearly surprised. 'Won't your mother be upset? You haven't been home in years.'

'I haven't come home to please my mother. I've come home for my son. This is between us, Fleur.'

'While I'm a Gilbert and you're a Hanover, it can never be just between us,' she said.

'You're a Hanover, too,' he reminded her, 'whether you regret it or not.'

He waited, half hoping, despite everything, that she would say that she didn't regret it. She swallowed, but said nothing. Foolish to expect otherwise.

'Understand that I'm serious about seeking custody of my son,' he said.

'Custody?' He saw the panic flare in her eyes. 'You really believe that you've any chance of getting that?'

'I'm sure of it. When your father is forced to file for bankruptcy and you lose your home, the court won't have any choice but to give him to me.'

'My father is not going bankrupt.'

He didn't respond.

'It's not going to happen, Matt. You abandoned me. Us.'

He bit down on the harsh words, the anger that he'd bottled up ever since he'd learned the truth; silence would serve him better.

'Access,' she said, and despite her attempt to keep calm he heard the fear eating away at her confidence. 'You'll get access, that's all. No court in the land would hand a little boy over to a father he doesn't know.'

'Are you sure? Given the choice between the good home I can offer and some bed-and-breakfast accommodation provided by the local authority for the homeless?'

'It's not going to happen,' she repeated, this time with the determination of a mother protecting her young.

He had to be careful. The last thing he wanted was to panic her. 'Maybe we can settle on a package deal,' he suggested. 'A divorce and our son in return for settlement of your debts?'

'I'm not interested in a divorce and you can't have our son.'

Despite everything, he found himself smiling. Not just any mother, but a tigress protecting a cub...

'Your negotiating skills could do with a little work, Fleur.'

'Your son is not a subject for negotiation.'

His son. Was she aware of what she'd said? That already she'd taken the first mental step towards giving him what he wanted?

'He already is,' he said. 'And you're the one who's making it so.' He allowed himself a smile. 'You're going to have to learn the art of compromise, Fleur. Tell me, what's the minimum you're prepared to offer?'

'Access,' she replied, just a touch desperately. 'You're entitled to that.'

'How much access? Every other weekend? Can I take him to Hungary for the summer? What about birthdays, Christmas?'

She went pale as she stared reality in the face. Swallowed, for a moment struggling to speak. But she didn't crumple or back down. 'He'll need time to get used to you,' she said. 'Tom must dictate the pace at which he's prepared to let you into his life.'

'Coached by you?'

'You left, Matt! You couldn't wait. Well, now you're going to have to. Tom will need time—'

'I suspect that you're the one who needs time, but I accept that these things can't be rushed. The cottage is the ideal place to spend some time together, all three of us, away from prying eyes, while Tom and I get to know one another.'

She frowned, but didn't suggest it was impossible. She just said, 'That wasn't what you said in your letter. Or when we spoke this morning.'

'I wanted to make sure I had your attention.'

'You've got it,' she assured him. 'You'd have had it any

time in the last six years if you'd ever bothered to put pen to paper or pick up a telephone.'

The sheer unfairness of that struck to the bone. 'Excuse me? I'm not the one who had a baby and didn't bother to tell her husband that he had a son.'

'When? How? By the time I realised that I was pregnant you'd disappeared off the face of the earth!'

'I begged you to come with me.'

'You *demanded* that I come with you,' she threw back at him. 'My mother was dying. My father was having a breakdown. I asked you to be patient. To wait.'

'The way I hear it, I'd still be waiting. And you'd still be creeping out to meet me on the odd night when he could spare you. Or when you could come up with a reasonable excuse. How many nights could you squeeze out of this Easter egg hunt, do you think? Or are they already spoken for?'

She shook her head, staring up into the rafters rather than meet his gaze. Swallowing hard, as if fighting back tears.

Who or what were they for? The girl she'd been? Lost dreams? Or because she couldn't hide any more? Because she would finally have to face the world with the truth.

What would she give him for another month?

Anything…

'If you'd been here,' she said, once she'd regained control, 'I'd have told my father everything.'

She closed her eyes for a moment, then dropped her gaze, looked directly at him, and it was Matt who found himself swallowing hard, his throat tight with regret.

'But you were gone, and with Hanovers on the market it seemed unlikely that you were ever going to come back—I seem to recall the words "hell" and "freezing over" featuring rather prominently in our last conversation.' She shrugged

'About Tom?'

'Of course about Tom. Even in the de[...] imagine he was mildly interested in the ide[...] of his first grandchild.'

'I told him the truth, Matt.'

He frowned. 'The truth? But I thought—'

'I told him that my pregnancy was the result of a meaningless one-night stand,' she said bitterly, remembering the look on her father's face as she'd handed him this second blow. 'Just one of those things that happens when you drink too much at an end of college party.'

'I don't believe you.'

No, well, she'd been fairly sure her father hadn't either, but that was none of his business. 'Why not? That is how long our marriage lasted. One night.'

'Excuse me? Unless you've divorced me for deserting you—and I'm fairly sure that you wouldn't have risked drawing attention to our marriage in that way—you're still my wife.'

'A technicality.'

'I think you'll find it counts, nonetheless.'

'It takes more than a piece of paper to make a marriage, Matt. Just as it takes more than a careless sperm donation to make a father.'

'You're right, but things are about to change. Bring Tom to the cottage to see me tomorrow after school and we can make a start on getting to know one another.'

'Tomorrow! But, I'm going to need time—'

'You've had time. Five years, two months, four days of it. It's all the time you're going to get.'

'Matt, please…'

'I'm being generous, Fleur. I could go to court tomorrow.

just turn up on your doorstep and demand my rights. Enlist your father's help.'

'Help? You think he'd help you?'

'I suspect that if he knew the truth he'd be a lot more understanding of my feelings than you appear to be.'

'No, that's not true. I do understand.' Of course she did. 'Please, Matt. Don't do anything rash. I don't know what the shock would do to him.'

'It's in your hands. Or did you think that all you had to do was smile at me nicely, say pretty please, and I'd just go away?'

'You've done it before,' she reminded him. She had to be strong. Of course Matt had rights, but they came a poor second to her little boy's happiness. 'How do I know you won't do it again? This is a child whose life you're about to overturn.' Not some woman who understood that people did things to hurt each other. That a broken heart was nothing in the great scheme of things. 'A little boy—'

'My child,' he cut in. 'My son!'

'Wrong pronoun, Matt. He does not belong to you. None of this is about you. It's about Tom. Walk back into his life and you'll belong to him, tied with an unbreakable cord. Understand that everything you do for the foreseeable future, you'll have to ask yourself, not "How will this affect my life?", but "How will it affect his?" First, last, always, he will have to come first. There will be no more "me."' She paused for breath. 'Maybe you should give some thought to your responsibilities instead of your precious rights while you can walk away, free, unencumbered, your own man.'

'Does that sound attractive to you?' He got to his feet, walked towards her, and it took all her courage to stand her ground as he looked into her eyes and asked, 'Is that what you long for, Fleur, in the dark hours of the night when you can't sleep? When you don't know where to turn to pay the bills? When there's no one to hold you and tell you that it'll be all right? To walk away, unencumbered, free to do whatever you want? Just say the word and it can all be yours.'

Did he believe it was that easy? She was a mother. There was no power strong enough to break the bond. She was a wife, too, and even now there were nights when she woke and, in that blissful moment before memory rushed back in, she reached for Matt. But to admit it would leave her utterly defenceless, completely at his mercy.

'Your mother's installed a webcam, has she?' she asked, doing her best to make a joke of it but, no longer able to face him off, she blinked and then looked at her watch as if to make the point that her time was limited.

He reached out and lifted her chin, forcing her to face him.

'I've worked hard, Fleur. I'm a rich man,' he said. 'I could make that happen for you. Give me what I want and I could make all your problems go away.'

CHAPTER FOUR

THE touch of Matt's fingers against her skin felt like a brand, as if he was marking her in some way, and his eyes burned into hers. Fleur was riveted to the floor, unable to move and, as if confident that all he had to do was offer the right incentive for her to crumble, he spread his hand, laying it against her cheek.

The gesture invited her to lean on him, surrender to a never-to-be-forgotten warmth, offering a promise that he would lift the burden from her shoulders, make the last six years go away.

For a moment she was tempted.

His touch evoked such tender memories. All the promise, the optimism of youth.

His closeness brought back the scent of the hay, crushed beneath their bodies, warm skin, clean sharp sweat...

She opened eyes that she hadn't been aware of closing and was jolted back to reality. This wasn't the boy she'd fallen in lust with. The young man who'd stolen her heart and persuaded her to do something that her head had always known was wrong.

This was a man whose presence exuded wealth, power.

She didn't know this Matthew Hanover.

But he thought he knew her. Touch the right buttons and

she'd do anything he wanted. Even surrender Tom. And it was because of Tom that he was here, not because of her. If he'd loved her enough, nothing—not her harsh words, his anger— would have kept him away for six long years.

The only reason he was here now, in this barn, talking to her instead of a lawyer, was because he thought he could jerk her strings, play on her emotions and bypass the slow grind of the courts. He was rich, he'd said. He could make all her problems go away and, looking at him, she had no reason to doubt him. But there would be a price. There was always a price to pay for mistakes, even those made with the best of intentions.

Above them the soft ghost-white whoosh of wings and a sifting of dust as a barn owl settled lightly on the beam broke the spell as they both looked up.

'It's good to see the barn isn't totally deserted,' Matt said, letting his hand fall to his side.

For a moment there he'd lost it.

For a moment, when she'd closed her eyes, her mouth softening as she'd momentarily leaned into his hand, on the point of accepting the refuge he'd so blindly offered, he thought she'd lost it, too. But it had only been for a moment. She'd already been taking a mental step back before the owl jolted her back to reality. He should be grateful that she'd let him off the hook. Years of driving himself, sleeping only when exhaustion left him no choice because his dreams were filled with her, years of holding on to his justified anger because to let it go left him with nothing—all that had been wiped out in an instant. But this close, remembering how it had once been, he couldn't quite bring himself to feel anything but regret.

'I have to go, Matt,' she said. 'I don't like to leave Dad for too long with Tom. He can be a bit of a handful.'

Well, that did it.

She'd put him firmly back in his place. Second—no, third in line now, after her father and her son.

His son.

Who was he kidding? She hadn't spent six years in a cold bed. She'd been discreet—she'd had years of practice at conducting an illicit liaison—but his agent had dug deep and found the connection to Charlie Fletcher. His gut twisted at the thought of her with him, but after six years what else did he expect?

'Nothing has been decided,' he pointed out.

'No. What did you expect?' she demanded, echoing his thoughts. 'Instant results? That's not going to happen, however you approach this.' She regarded him levelly. Thoughtfully. 'And once the law gets involved you'll have to do everything by the book.'

Was she trying to turn the tables? Threaten him? Foolish, foolish...

'I'm well aware of that, Fleur.'

If all he'd wanted was access to the boy, he'd have called a lawyer long-distance from Hungary in January, put the wheels in motion and left her to deal with the inevitable fallout on her own. It wasn't enough. He intended to make her pay personally for the five years he'd lost.

'I was sure you would be,' she said. 'You never could wait for anything, could you, Matt?' Then, 'Maybe it would be better, after all, to leave it to the courts.'

She was bluffing. 'Including the blood test?' he asked.

She visibly flinched, as he'd known she would. She had a needle phobia, had been a nervous wreck when she'd had to have a tetanus booster. He'd teased her about it, bought her chocolate, said that if she put a piece in her mouth and thought of him while the needle went in she wouldn't feel a thing. Practising had certainly taken her mind off it for a while…

Now he wondered if Tom had inherited her fear, or been infected by it. Or was it that, as a mother, she felt the anguish, the fear, twice over?

'Maybe we can sort something out tomorrow afternoon,' he said.

'Tomorrow?'

'Old Cottage, Upper Haughton,' he prompted. 'You're going to bring Tom, remember?'

'I'm afraid that won't be possible. Tom has a play date tomorrow after school.' She managed a smile. Relief, he thought, at having a legitimate excuse, rather than amusement that he was forced to stand in line for his son's time. 'He has a much better social life than I do.'

'Is that right?' She didn't know it yet, but it was about to pick up. 'Then I guess I'll have to make do with your company.'

'No, Matt. It's the only time I have to…'

She didn't finish the sentence.

To what? It was the only time she had to get laid? No. He wasn't going to the back of that queue.

'Think of it as your own play date,' he said abruptly. 'If your social life is so empty, I'd have thought you'd be grateful for the outing.'

'I was going to use the opportunity to go into Maybridge to stock up at the supermarket. It's easier without a child in tow.'

'How can I possibly compete with that?' he asked cynically.

She shook her head once, as if his sarcasm wasn't worth any other response. Maybe she was right. Then, visibly gathering herself, she said, 'I thought you might feel that way about it. It's why I didn't want to say where I was going. But you're right, Matt. We need to talk about this like civilised adults, not kids hiding in an old barn. The shopping will have to wait.'

'No,' he said before he could stop himself. 'I haven't forgotten what it takes to run a place like Gilberts. No doubt every moment of your day is spoken for.' He dug inside his coat, took out his wallet and a pen, wrote an email address on the reverse of one of his business cards. 'E-mail me a list of what you want and I'll see that it's waiting for you tomorrow afternoon.' Then, because he didn't want her to think he was going soft on her, 'That way you'll have an excuse in hand for another day.'

Ignoring his gibe, she said, 'You'd do my shopping for me? You must be desperate.'

'I said it'll be waiting for you, Fleur. I've got better things to do with my time than push a trolley around a supermarket.'

That had put her right in her place, Fleur thought. They'd started out life as equals. Each of them heir to generations of nurserymen, with the same acreage, history, store of knowledge at their command. The same future ahead of them: college, some time working for the large-scale plant nurseries where they could gain experience to take back to their own family firms. The same family tragedy to contend with. The only difference was that she was a woman, tied to hearth and home, her role to care for the sick and the young, hold things together, the way that women always had throughout history, while Matt had the freedom to walk away, build himself a new empire, a new life somewhere else.

While Tom was as much his son as hers, she was the one who'd been left holding the baby, struggling to keep things ticking over on her own when her father, sunk in the depths of despair, hadn't cared what happened to the business.

Matt, even now, didn't even have to put himself out to get her shopping so that she could spare him two precious hours of her time. He would pay someone else to do it for him.

She looked at the card he'd given her, which was lying beside her keyboard as she tried to remember everything she needed. She'd come so close to telling him what to do with his personal shopper, but he was right, no matter how much his nasty little dig had hurt. It was the perfect cover for their meeting, giving her one more day's grace before she had to own up, tell her father the truth, see the look in his eyes as he understood that it hadn't only been his wife who had been betraying him all those years ago.

Matt compared the list he was holding, its insistence upon economy brands, with the shelves in front of him. Every inclination was to ignore what Fleur had written and go for the best quality, the most expensive labels. He didn't care about Seth Gilbert, had long ago forced himself not to think about Fleur; he did care about his son. He should be eating the best food that money could buy.

Unfortunately, he'd allowed her to believe that someone else would be following her instructions—someone who was just doing a job and who would, presumably, buy exactly what was on the list. Besides, she was going to insist on paying for whatever he bought and clearly her budget only ran to 'economy.'

He'd thought, when he discovered he had a son he knew nothing about, that he'd felt shut out, excluded. Standing in front of a supermarket shelf, unable to make the simplest of decisions about which can of beans to buy, brought home to him more fully than anything that had happened in the last few weeks the true meaning of his exclusion from his son's life.

His bankers were already putting together a trust fund, ensuring that, no matter what happened, Tom's future would be secure, but this was about the every-penny-counts, day-to-day care of the boy. Because of her stubbornness, the fact that she cared more about not upsetting her father than for the welfare of his son, she had never gone after the maintenance payments she was entitled to. She'd denied Tom the best possible start in life.

All that was about to change, he decided as, making an executive decision, he tossed the expensive stuff into the trolley. It would give him pleasure to see her sweat as she wrote him a cheque for it—and she would insist on it. With luck it would bring her to her senses more quickly.

If it didn't, he was sure a good lawyer would be able to use her shopping list as ammunition against her if it came to a fight.

Upper Haughton was the ideal hideaway. A scant ten miles from Longbourne, but light years from it in style, the road through it led nowhere, but looped around the picture-perfect village green before pottering off down lanes that narrowed to footpaths. No one was going to drive by and spot her Land Rover where it had no right to be.

As Fleur drove past the mixture of ancient cottages and large, well-kept houses it occurred to her that even renting a hovel in a place like this must cost telephone numbers.

Old Cottage, with its pie-crust gables and its deep covered porch with benches on either side of the door, was anything but a hovel. On the contrary, with its flower-filled garden and the swing hanging from the branch of a vast old apple tree, it looked like something out of a storybook.

When Matt had said he was rich, she decided, he had not been exaggerating.

She parked outside the fence and lowered herself to the ground. She'd made a little more effort with her appearance today, but only because she was supposed to be going into town. Her trousers and sweater had been bought at the church jumble sale, but they were better quality than anything she could have bought new. Her shirt might have come from the local market, but it was clean, freshly ironed and, lacking the resources for a hairdresser, she'd brushed her hair until it shone and fastened it at the nape of her neck in a wide clip that Tom had bought her for Christmas—also from the jumble sale.

Her image pretty much matched that of any young comfortably off country mother of her acquaintance. She was wearing their cast-offs, after all.

By the time she'd locked the car door—she was just putting off the moment for as long as possible, since she didn't for a moment believe that anyone in their right mind would want to steal it—and opened the gate, Matt was standing in the open doorway, waiting for her.

'You're late,' he said as she walked self-consciously along a short path lined with sweet-scented wallflowers towards him. 'I was beginning to think I was going to have to come and fetch you.'

'I was delayed by a phone call.'

'And if it had been Tom who was waiting for you? Would you still have put the phone call first?'

'No, but—'

'But it was someone chasing you for payment and you had to soothe their worries.'

She considered telling him the truth, that it was someone

placing an order, but she doubted that he'd believe her, so she didn't bother. Instead she said, 'I knew you'd understand about putting business before pleasure.'

'This *is* business.' He stood back to let her in.

'If you think that, we have nothing to say to one another,' she said, ignoring his unspoken invitation to step inside. 'What we're about to decide will affect my son's emotional welfare—'

'Wrong pronoun, Fleur.'

Well, at least he'd taken that message on board.

'Try *our*,' he suggested. 'He's *our* son.'

Damn!

She'd been so determined to show him that she was not going to fight him if he wanted to be a real parent, to spend time, give love rather than money. Win his trust. She'd even been practising using the word 'our', so alien to her, so foreign...

Her nerves in shreds, she'd failed at the first hurdle.

Not that he'd done anything to earn inclusion in the possessive.

'You're still getting it wrong, Matt. We're *his* parents.'

He came close to a smile then. As if he'd got everything he wanted from the exchange. 'You've had five years to get the words right, Fleur. You'll have to be patient with me while I catch up. Come in.' He led the way, apparently confident that she'd follow him. Then, perhaps sensing her hesitation, he turned back and said, 'Stay or go, presumably you'll want your shopping.'

Of course she would. Clever Matt.

She stepped through the front door of the cottage, closed it behind her and followed him into the kind of sitting room she'd once dreamed they'd share. It wasn't freshly minted, nothing was new—far from it—but everything, from the log fire burning brightly in the hearth to the roomy sofa set square in front of it, offered comfort, an invitation to sit down, curl up and forget the world outside.

'This is lovely,' she said, dropping her bag on the sofa and crossing to the fire to warm her hands. 'You were lucky to find something this good at such short notice.'

'It would be more accurate to say that it found me.' She turned to look at him. 'I sat next to the owner on the plane home. We got chatting. I mentioned I was looking for somewhere and she offered me this, if I wanted it.'

She?

'Well, that's…handy.' She did her best to ignore the way her guts clenched at the thought of him sharing confidences with some glamorous—make that rich and glamorous—woman over the champagne in first class. Sitting side by side. Close enough to touch… Then, because it seemed so unlikely, she asked, 'She offered you her spare cottage just like that? A complete stranger? How long does it take to fly from Hungary?'

'Two and a half hours.'

'As long as that?' she said, trying but failing to keep the sarcasm from her voice.

'You can get to know a lot about someone, sitting next to them for a couple of hours.' This time his smile made it all the way up to his eyes. 'Apparently the cottage has been empty since Christmas, when the previous tenant got married. Amy said I'd be doing her a favour keeping it aired.'

'You must have made quite an impression.'

'It wasn't as if I was a total stranger,' he replied. 'She buys all her gardening supplies from Hanovers.'

'I buy all my groceries from the supermarket on the Maybridge Road,' she retorted, 'but I can't imagine giving the manager the run of the house just because the service is so good.'

'No? Oh, well, I suppose I must just have the kind of face that inspires trust.'

'That must be it. She lives locally, then?'

'On the other side of the green.'

Suddenly everything dropped into place. And no, she didn't think it was his face that his landlady was interested in. Nor did she want to know what other favours he'd be doing for *Amy*.

Not that it was any of her business.

It was years since he'd left and, no matter how painful the thought, it seemed unlikely that he'd felt bound by vows they'd made, no matter how fervent, so long ago.

It had been easier for her. Not that there hadn't been interest. She might be a single mother, but that hadn't put off some really quite nice men who'd asked her out. But, even if she'd been interested, her life was already complicated enough.

But alone, far from home, it would be unreasonable to expect Matt to remain celibate just because of an ill-advised union.

'She lives in the big white house you can just see behind the high wall as you drive into the village,' he added, as if she was the slightest bit interested.

'Convenient,' she said, straightening. 'She'll be able to keep a neighbourly eye on you. Make sure you don't throw any rowdy parties, at least not without inviting her.'

A thoughtful smile flickered across Matt's face, warning her that she'd said too much. Betrayed her thoughts.

'I wouldn't dream of throwing any kind of party without inviting her,' he said. 'This is a friendly place. I've already had a visitor. Kay Ravenscar, the woman who used to live here, dropped in with a pot of home-made marmalade and an invitation to dinner. She runs a garden contract business, so she knows my mother too.'

'A real home from home for you then. Of course a single man living in a place like this will always be in great demand.'

'Except, of course, that I'm not single.'

'In all but the details.'

'You'll find, Fleur, that I'm something of a stickler for the details, which is why I accepted for both of us. This Friday. Seven-thirty for eight.' Then, before she had time to object, he said, 'Can I get you anything? Tea? Coffee?'

She didn't want either, but sensing that it would be easier to talk if they had something to distract them, she said, 'Tea, thank you.'

'Why don't you come through and check out your groceries while I make it?' he suggested.

'I'm sure they're perfect,' she said, but snatched up her bag and followed him into the kitchen. It would be a lot easier talking over a mug with the kitchen table between them than sharing that sofa. 'I'll pay you now and put them in the back of the Rover.'

She'd been certain that he'd tell her not to bother; he was, after all, five years behind with maintenance payments. She didn't want them, but she was fairly certain that his first method of attack would be financial. He'd already brought up the fact that the business was in debt; maybe he thought she'd respond to a little fiscal inducement. While she couldn't—wouldn't—do anything to stop him making financial provision for Tom's future, she wasn't about to allow him to underwrite her grocery bill and she was ready to tell him that.

'You'll find the receipt in one of the boxes,' he said, as he clicked on the kettle, reached for a couple of mugs.

Oh, right. Maybe this wasn't going to be as difficult as she'd anticipated. Glad they weren't going to start with an argument, she picked up the till roll to check the total before she got out her purse. Unless the price of basic essentials had increased dramatically in the last month—or he was charging her for the cost of a personal shopper—it was way out, and she turned to the boxes, picking out a couple of tins at random.

Neither.

'It's none of my business,' she said, 'but if you want my advice you won't use the same woman to do your shopping again.'

He turned. 'There's a problem?'

'Only with the details,' she said drily, searching through the boxes, but not finding what she was looking for. 'She doesn't appear to understand the word "economy". Where's the list I sent you?'

'Isn't it there?'

Something in his voice warned her that he was well aware that the list and shopping did not match.

'No, Matt, it isn't. I suggest you print off another copy. You'll need it when you call her and explain why she has to take these things back for a refund.' She put her purse back in her bag, slung it over her shoulder and said, 'Forget the tea. And the chat. I have to go and do the job myself, properly.'

'No. Wait.' Then, 'Don't go.'

She waited.

'I don't want you giving Tom "economy" anything.'

'What makes you think I am?'

'Cheap tea, cheap coffee, white bread. And are you feeding the child exclusively on baked beans?'

'For your information, Matt, Tom isn't allowed coffee. And he doesn't like baked beans.'

'He doesn't?' Not sure what to say, he gestured towards the boxes. 'But—'

'But next week I have the packers in to despatch the mini plug orders. They start early, and part of the deal is that I give them breakfast. Of course, if you're so concerned about them that you're prepared to underwrite the extra expense, I'll feed them premium beans and have the butcher deliver prime back, his best sausages and organic free-range eggs instead of the standard fare, and bill those to you as well.'

He shrugged. 'Maybe we should leave it at the beans and the bread.'

'Just the beans, actually. I like to support the village baker, but the bread can go in the freezer for emergencies.' He frowned. 'I gave the packing girls wholemeal toast once without thinking. They suggested it tasted like straw.'

'I'll bet they weren't that polite.'

'I gave you the edited version.'

Matt dropped a couple of tea bags into a pot. He'd made a fool of himself for no good reason and he couldn't for the life of him see a way to regain the advantage.

She gave it back to him. There was the lightest touch on his arm and she said, 'It was a good start, Matt. Caring. Thoughtful.'

Unprepared for approval, he turned but she was already counting out cash for the groceries, carefully flicking each note before laying it on the table.

'You don't have to—'

'Don't worry,' she said, 'I'm not.' As if sensing his confusion, she finally looked up. 'Since you clearly did the shopping yourself, Matt, I'm letting you off the hook.'

'Oh?' Then, realising that he'd been rumbled, he said

hastily, 'I couldn't get anyone at such short notice. I thought you might need some of the stuff straight away.'

'I was sure that was it,' she said, going back to counting out notes on to the table. 'I'm afraid I can only pay you for the economy versions I asked for.' She paused, glanced up. 'Of course, if you'd rather take it all back and change it, so that you're not out of pocket…?'

'No!' He'd wanted to make her sweat, feel the pinch. He wanted to punish her for the last five years. He wanted her on her knees begging for his help, but she wasn't playing and now he just felt mean. He wanted to tell her to put her money back in her purse, but knew instinctively that that was no longer an option. She'd won this round. 'No,' he repeated. 'It was my mistake. I'll stand the difference. I just hope your packers appreciate it.'

'Sorry. By the time they've plastered on the tomato ketchup they won't notice the difference,' she said.

And then she smiled.

It was a repeat of that heart-stopping moment when he'd first glimpsed her through a crowd at a party. Not that it was the first time he'd seen her. She'd been there most of his life. His bedroom window had overlooked the Gilbert garden and he'd seen her there, a little carrot-topped kid playing on her swing, a long-limbed tomboy climbing up to her tree-house, a teen lying in the grass with a book, dawdling through the village on her way home when she'd got off the bus after school. They'd never spoken in all those years, but that night he'd gone up to her and said, 'If I forget who you are, will you forget who I am and dance with me?'

She'd smiled then and said, 'I thought you'd never ask.'

CHAPTER FIVE

THE click of the kettle switching itself off brought Matt back to the kitchen, the present.

'I'll put these in the Rover,' Fleur said, reaching for one of the boxes.

'If I were to suggest swapping roles,' he said, 'you make the tea, I carry the boxes, would you be totally outraged?'

'Oh, please.' Her laugh was a hollow thing, but she straightened, leaving the groceries where they were. 'I'm long past that kind of pathetic nonsense, but if it bothers you, Matt, you could avoid any suggestion of sexual stereotyping by doing both jobs. You won't get any argument from me. Believe me, if life were simpler I'd take you home with me to unpack the boxes and put the stuff away, too.'

'You're the one making it complicated.'

'If I'd been looking for a simple life, I'd have said no when you first asked me to dance.'

'Your call,' he said, with a shrug that suggested he didn't give a damn. But he'd just had a glimpse of what her life must be like. Doing everything. Responsible for everything. What the hell was the matter with Seth Gilbert? His wife had been having an affair. It happened. His mother had suffered, too, but she'd pulled herself out of it, got on with life. Not before she'd wrecked the future he'd planned, though. But at least he'd been able to start again. Fleur hadn't that option. 'Just say the word, Fleur, and I'll be right there.'

'Thanks for the offer, but by my calculation it's about six years too late.' For a moment she held his gaze, as if daring him to deny it. He didn't, but she was the first to blink, look away, making a performance out of searching in her pocket for her keys. She tossed them to him and said, 'Go ahead, flex your muscles while I do the little woman bit.'

He was in no hurry, and realising she'd have to squeeze past him to get to the kettle, she took the long way around the table.

'I've never been inside your house,' he said. 'Not even when your parents were out.'

'We ran enough risks to be together.'

'Did we? Did you?'

She picked up the teapot, poured in some hot water to warm it, sloshing it around, keeping her hands busy, doing anything but look at him, answer his questions, because, while he'd stuck to the pledge they'd made, that nothing would keep them apart, Fleur knew she'd been the one who'd refused at the final hurdle.

The pot warm, there was nothing else she could do until he moved so that she could tip the water into the sink.

'Is that how you want to play it now?' he pressed. 'Like this? Sneaking around, still keeping even the fact that we know one another a secret?'

'No...'

She shook her head as if even thinking about it was more than she could cope with, and there was something so forlorn, so lonely in the gesture that Matt took the teapot from her, using the excuse to turn away as he emptied it into the sink.

Giving himself time to steel himself against a longing to hold her, to reassure her, so intense he thought he might die of it. He'd come for his son, not to rekindle a romance with a girl who'd been too weak to stand beside him when he'd needed her.

'No,' she repeated, as if trying to convince herself.

'We're not kids any more, Fleur.' She didn't bother to reply and he stared out of the window at the perfectly kept kitchen garden. Everything neat and tidy. If only life were as simple. 'Shakespeare had it all wrong you know,' he said. 'There would have been no reconciliation. The death of Romeo and Juliet would have simply plunged their families into more blame, more blood-letting.'

'I don't see much comparison between our parents' affair and Romeo and Juliet, to be honest.'

'No?' He shook his head. 'Maybe I'm getting it out of proportion.'

'Maybe. But thankfully we live in a civilised English village. The worst we have to contend with are battles over planning permission.' She paused. 'So far.'

'That's up to you, Fleur. I'm not dragging Tom into our sordid world of secrets and lies.'

He didn't have to be looking at her to know that she'd flinched.

'Our son is five years old, Matt. He doesn't know how to keep a secret. He hasn't learned to tell lies and I'm not going to give him his first lesson. The minute he knows about you, so will everyone in his world.'

'So we have to make sure that our parents know first.'

'Yes.' He waited for her to offer some idea of how that might be achieved without blood on the carpet. She'd had a full twenty-four hours to think about it. 'That's what I'm telling you.'

'So? What shall we do? Invite them both over for tea and a little game of Truth, Dare, Kiss or Promise?'

'Don't be flippant,' she snapped.

'I'm open to better suggestions.'

'No, Matt. This is all new to you and you want to claim what's yours and damn everyone else's feelings. I've lived with this since the day I realised I was pregnant. All I'm asking you to do is to hold off for a few more weeks.'

She took half a step back as he spun round, but his emotions were fully under control now. It was easy when he was faced with reality. The fact that while he had to fight to keep himself from reaching out to her, offering comfort, all she wanted him to do was go away and let her carry on in her own sweet way.

Tough.

It wasn't going to happen.

'Give me one good reason why I should,' he demanded. 'What difference does it make whether the bombshell hits now or in a month's time? The shock isn't going to be any less.'

'I have to get Dad through Chelsea. It's the only hope he has of regaining his pride. After that...'

'After that?'

'One way or the other, everything will have changed.'

'Why? What's so special about Chelsea?'

'We're relaunching Gilbert Fuchsias,' she said, but whereas a moment ago she was meeting his gaze head on, suddenly she wasn't. 'If we can just hold on until then...'

'What?'

She shook her head, apparently more interested in the state of her shoes than in him, so that he was looking down at her. He had the notion that if he stopped this, if instead of fighting her he just reached out, put his arms around her, brushed her hair with his lips, that all the years would be wiped out, they'd be back to that moment when they'd first met.

Eighteen-year-old Fleur Gilbert had come into his arms as if it was the one place she'd always wanted to be and he'd held her as if she were the only woman in the world. In the space of a heartbeat, while he'd pressed his cheek against her hair and she'd laid her head against his shoulder, their lives had changed for ever.

Was she remembering that moment, too? Doing it on purpose? Keeping her head down, hoping that his hormones would kick in as they had done all those years ago? That once she had him in her arms, her bed, he'd promise her anything?

That had been his plan.

He'd been a faithful husband to an absent wife for the best part of six years. He'd been ready to make her pay for that. Surrender her body, then surrender her son. And then he'd walk away and she'd be the one who'd lost everything.

Making plans in the cold light of day, driven by pain and anger fuelled with the information that flowed in about his son, his wife, it had seemed so easy. Anger had been the single emotion that had driven him for so long. Then he'd flown home and somehow he'd found himself telling the woman in the seat beside him the whole story. Showing her a photograph of Fleur that he'd kept, despite everything. Remembering how it had been. How much he had loved her. How much he had lost…

Since then nothing had been simple.

Writing the letter that would bring her racing to offer him anything had proved the first obstacle.

He'd intended to write it by hand. Make it really personal. His hand had refused to co-operate, the shaky letters betraying a different emotion, one he was determined to keep damped down, hidden, and he'd been forced to type the wretched thing.

'If we can hold on until then…?' he repeated. *What?* 'Is that what you asked the bank manager for today?' he asked, doing his best to concentrate on reality. 'Time?'

His hormones were going to hate him for it, but he forced the words out, determined to break the spell, refusing to repeat the same mistakes, go round for ever, caught in the trap they'd woven about themselves.

'To hold off calling in the receivers until the end of May?' he continued, pushing her for an answer.

Her head came up, eyes wide with shock. 'How do you know that I was at the bank?'

Well, that got her hair out of her eyes. Grabbed her attention.

'An educated guess. It's common knowledge that you're in financial trouble and this morning when you left the house you were wearing a suit, carrying a briefcase.'

'Oh, well. Case proved.' Then, as his words sank in, 'You were spying on me!'

'Not spying. I was watching from the window, waiting for you to take Tom to school. I wanted to see him, Fleur.'

Her hand flew to cover her mouth as if she realised just how that must have been, to catch the first glimpse of the boy from an upstairs window, a hundred yards and a high fence between them. Unable to reach out a helping hand, boost him up into the seat beside his mother, ruffle his hair, tell him to work hard, have fun. A distant spectator in his son's life.

'I'm sorry,' she said. 'I'm so sorry.'

'How bad is it, Fleur?' he asked, cutting off her apology.

She'd spoken nothing but the truth, after all. He had paid people to check up on her. To find information he could use to get what he wanted. He'd chosen his words with the precise intention of making her feel wretched and he'd succeeded.

She shook her head, eyes closed as if to keep back tears she didn't want him to see. Only when she had herself back under control did she say, 'It would be so much easier if your mother would get off our case. Why does she hate us so much?' She made a gesture as if to suggest she could understand why he might hate her, but that this was different. 'Your father was as much to blame as my mother for what happened.'

'Your mother was driving. She was drunk.'

'They were both drunk!' Then, 'I'm not excusing what she did, but she didn't just lose her licence. She lost her life, not in an instant, but horribly, knowing that if she did survive, all she had to look forward to was pain, disability. And no matter how badly she behaved, it doesn't explain why your mother seems to hold Dad personally responsible for what happened.'

'She doesn't. It would be ridiculous.' Then, recalling their conversation the previous morning, 'Did he object to her application for planning permission to build houses on the Hanover land?'

'What?' She shook her head. 'Dad wasn't doing much of anything at the time.'

'You, then?'

'Nobody asked my opinion. I'm not the landowner, or at least I wasn't then. But nobody needed to ask me. A housing estate tacked on its outskirts would have completely changed the nature of the village. Everyone was against it. There was even a petition in the post office.'

'I'd probably have signed it myself,' he assured her. 'But if you'd been in her shoes, desperate to sell up and escape, who would you have blamed?'

'She must know the truth, Matt. If not then, now. All she'd have to do is ask her pals on the Parish Council.'

'Now who's being paranoid?' She shrugged. 'She's moved on. Made a new life.'

'I know, and I admire her for that…'

'But?'

'But I just wish she'd concentrate on her business, her committees, her visits to expensive health farms, and leave us alone.'

'Health farms?'

'She looks younger now than she did when your father was alive. Call me cynical, but I'd suggest she was getting a little help.'

'What exactly has she done, apart from offer to buy you out?' he asked, refusing to go there.

'For peanuts.' She shrugged. 'To be honest, it's more the wearing drip-feed of small complaints. Nothing new there, but I suspect you might be right about the planning permission thing. Tit for tat. We had an offer for the barn last year from a local builder who wanted to turn it into holiday cottages. It would have solved a lot of problems. We were turned down flat.'

'You could appeal.'

'It takes time and money and, as you already appear to know, we have neither. And the builder survives on the goodwill of the PC.' Fleur glanced at him. 'Maybe, now you're home, you could ask her to play nice.'

'Introduce her to her grandson and maybe she'd listen.'

'Are you suggesting that she'd welcome me into the family with open arms?' She laughed, but it wasn't a pretty sound. 'If she knew that Tom was her grandson, Matt, she wouldn't lift a finger to give us breathing space. On the contrary, your mother would move heaven and earth to crush Gilberts. She'd do anything to ensure that you got custody.'

Remembering the casual way that she'd offered him the Gilbert house, Matt suspected Fleur was right. But it didn't make sense. His mother was, after all, only a Hanover by marriage. There had to be more to it than an ongoing feud. And why were the Gilberts in financial straits? They'd been in business a long time; the land was theirs. What had happened to their capital reserves?

'She's not alone in that, is she, Matt?' Fleur said, interrupting this train of thought. 'It's what you said in your letter. You're going for custody.'

There was no anger in Fleur's voice. No bluster. She was just telling it how it was.

'If you think these private meetings are going to help you get that, then you're mistaken. You'd be better off spending the time with a lawyer.'

'I want...' Damn! It had all been so clear in his mind. Simple. Straightforward. People complicated things. 'I want what's best for my son,' he said.

She finally managed a smile. 'Well, at least we're both starting from the same place.' Then, with a shrug, 'Of course, if Dad could sell the barn, we'd be on a slightly more even playing field.'

'I'm sorry, Fleur. I can't help you there. My mother has plans of her own for the place.'

'I beg your pardon? Plans? She doesn't even own it.'

'She wants to turn it into a restaurant. Once you've been forced to file for bankruptcy. She's got the plans drawn up.

Actually, you've all done her a big favour in making sure that land at that end of the village can't be used for development. She'll be able to buy at agricultural prices.'

'And then persuade her pals to support her planning appeal? I'll burn the barn down first,' she declared, outraged.

'Let me know when and I'll loan you a box of matches.' She frowned, obviously confused. 'With you in jail for arson, Fleur, Tom's custody won't be in question.'

'Oh, please. You think arson would be suspected? Anyone with half an eye could see that it's been used as a lovers' haunt. A lamp could be so easily upset in a moment of passion.' She made a dismissive gesture, as if wishing she hadn't brought it up. 'I don't have to draw you a picture, do I?'

'No, my memory is in full working order.'

It was a long time since their trysts in the barn, but the pictures in his head were still as vivid as if it had all happened yesterday.

'All that dry straw lying about,' she went on a little desperately. Maybe she didn't want to remember either. 'It would go up in an instant.'

'My offer of help still stands if you need to make it look convincing.'

She let out a puff of outraged breath.

'Unless you have someone else lined up?' She frowned, as if she had no idea what he was talking about and he let it go. 'Is it well insured?'

'The barn? Good grief, no.' Then, catching on, 'Are you suggesting that I've considered burning it down for the insurance?' she demanded, although whether that was causing her outrage, or his suggestion that they re-enact love's young dream on the shabby sofa in pursuit of credibility, he couldn't have said.

'You seem to have it all worked out. But if it's not insured...'

'It's not.'

'Then obviously fraud couldn't be a motive. Even so, I'd advise you not to do anything hasty. The way things are going we might need it for a week or two yet.'

'What?' Then, as his words sank in, 'No. I planned my life once on that sofa, Matt. I'm not doing it again. Last night was it. I'm never setting foot in the place—'

'Never say never,' he warned.

'All future discussions will take place in daylight. In a lawyer's office if necessary.'

'Fine. If that's what you want, Fleur, we'll do it by the book.' He finally moved, picked up one of the boxes. 'Do you want to get the door?'

'And if...' She didn't move, just swallowed, taking several attempts to get out the words. 'And if I didn't...'

'What?'

'Want to do it by the book.'

'You don't,' he pointed out. 'If you'd wanted that you wouldn't have come to the barn last night. You wouldn't be here now.' She didn't say anything. Didn't deny it. 'You want time. Not for yourself, not even for Tom, but for your father. Why am I surprised? You always did put him first.'

'That's not true!'

The words exploded from her, her green eyes flashed. It was a pretty performance.

'Lie to yourself if you want to, Fleur, but don't try it on me.' And, having silenced her, he said, 'Tell me what's so important about Chelsea.'

She shook her head, wrapped her arms around her waist, as if protecting herself. Putting up a barrier between them. 'I can't do that.'

'If you want time, you've going to have to.'

'I promised—'

'You promised your father? How sweet.' Every time they seemed to be making progress, to be within reach of accord, she reminded him that when it really counted he was at the back of the queue. 'You made a promise to me once. You managed to break that one easily enough.'

Fleur, finding this closeness more difficult than she could ever have imagined, closed her eyes and drew in a deep breath, refusing to blurt out that he was being unfair, that she hadn't broken her promise. Not the one about being faithful to him, even until death, anyway, but maybe he was judging her by his own standards. She didn't say that either. This could so easily become a fight and that would help no one, least of all Tom.

Instead she concentrated on what mattered.

'You know how it is in this business, Matt. The tiniest whisper and it'll be round the plant world faster than white fly through a glasshouse.'

'There was a time you'd have trusted me enough to tell me anything.'

'There was a time when I believed you'd never walk out on me,' she shot back at him.

So much for biting her tongue, keeping the past out of it.

'I didn't walk out on you. You chose to stay behind.'

'You think I had a *choice*?'

For a moment they stood facing one another across the kitchen. They were both breathing a little harder than necessary, considering they hadn't moved. Then Matt shifted the box and, tucking it up beneath one arm, opened the door himself.

Left alone in the kitchen, Fleur let out a juddering sigh.

Then, because she had to do something to occupy her hands, distract herself, she hunted for tea bags and, while Matt made a couple more journeys to load up her shopping, she made the tea.

When the last box was stowed and he was standing somewhere behind her, still waiting for an answer to his question, a reason why he should give her the time she needed, she said, 'My father believes he's bred a pure yellow fuchsia.'

The only response was a seemingly endless silence and finally she turned round to face him. His face, his body language was unreadable.

'And you, Fleur?' he asked her finally. 'What do you believe?'

So. He'd picked up on doubts she could barely bring herself to think, let alone voice. Well, of course, if she'd been certain, if she'd seen it with her own eyes, she'd have said, 'My father *has* bred a pure yellow fuchsia.' She wouldn't have been able to contain her excitement.

'I didn't even know he'd applied for a place in the marquee at Chelsea until the letter came from the Royal Horticultural Society,' she admitted. 'We haven't shown anywhere since before the accident. I've tried to interest him in the smaller shows, anything to get him out, mixing with people he's known all his life. Nothing doing. It would never have occurred to me to go for the big one.' She lifted her shoulders, then let them fall. 'If it's all pie in the sky,' she said, 'your mother will be able to extend to her heart's content. And have her restaurant. We'll be a laughing stock. Finished.'

He nodded as if satisfied, and well he might be.

'I'll give you Chelsea, Fleur. You have until the end of May, but there'll be no more time after that. Tomorrow I'll lodge letters with my solicitors to be sent to your father and my mother on the last day of May, telling them everything.'

'Matt—'

'I haven't finished,' he said. 'You've asked me to wait for my son. I want something in return.'

'Anything,' she said, eager to demonstrate that she appreciated what he was doing. The sacrifice he was making.

He reached out, touched her lips with his fingertips. 'Anything?' he repeated, so softly that she might almost have imagined it. But his eyes darkened, the very air stilled.

His touch was still magic, sending intense, luscious waves of desire swirling out from the point of contact until every centimetre of her skin was tingling, alive, responsive to an irresistible siren call.

His mouth followed his fingers, tracing the outline of her lips, then his tongue stole the bones from her limbs and she was limp in his arms, beyond thought, as his breath, soft and warm, brushed against her cheek, as his hands cradled her head as if she were rare porcelain.

How often had she lived this moment, dreamed of it, yearned for just this touch as he tormented her, made her wait, reducing her to begging mush?

She did not know how she'd had the strength to resist him, do her duty, when he'd demanded that she leave with him the day after his father's funeral. Maybe if he hadn't been so angry. If he'd been prepared to listen, to take his time, to talk to her instead of just insisting she choose. Maybe if he'd touched her then, as he was touching her now…

A guttural sound escaped her lips. Need, desire…

'Anything?' he murmured again.

'Yes, yes…' And then she realised that he'd eased back an inch, that he wasn't making love to her, that the only contact between them was his hands cradling her head, his thumbs tormenting the line of her jaw, brushing against an ear.

This wasn't some precious memory she was conjuring up out of the past but a callous proposition, and Matt was waiting for an answer to the question he'd just posed with his mouth, his body, his hands.

'Are you suggesting that I sleep with you in return for your patience?' she asked, wanting to be absolutely sure what he was asking, her voice even, low—she'd had years, after all, to practise keeping her feelings under wraps.

'Sleep?' he returned, soft as a baby's breath. 'Could you actually spare the time to sleep with me?'

'You just want sex, then?'

'You're my wife, Fleur.'

He wanted to punish her, she thought. He wanted to punish her for not loving him enough to leave her dying mother, her poor broken father, a business falling apart.

If he still had any feelings for her, the tiniest remembrance of how they had once loved one another, he wouldn't be able to do that.

And with that realisation something inside her shattered. It couldn't be her heart. She knew it couldn't be that because her heart had been dismantled bit by bit. The day she'd told her father she was pregnant—and wouldn't, couldn't tell him who Tom's father was. The day her baby had been born and Matt hadn't been there to hold her hand or to lift his son high as a proud father should. The day she'd registered his birth, leaving a blank space where Matt's name should have been. Each day since, watching her son grow, knowing that Matt was missing his first step, first word, first day at school. Each day that he hadn't come home.

This was different. All through those years she'd lived with the belief that one day he'd walk up to the front door.

No apology, no explanations—she wouldn't have asked for either—he'd just be there.

What had shattered, she realised, was hope.

She knocked his hands away and, without a word she picked up her bag, walked out of the door, down the path. For some reason the catch on the gate took forever to open. It didn't matter. She had forever.

Then she reached the Land Rover, grabbed the handle and wrenched on it. It didn't budge. She leaned her forehead against the door, taking deep breaths. She wouldn't cry. She'd learned the hard way how to keep a lid on her emotions. But this time it was harder than she could ever have dreamed.

'Hello? Are you all right? Can I do anything?'

For a moment she didn't move. She spent the time fitting herself back together, shoving the pain back into its box. Then, and only then, did she turn, polite smile in place, ready to face the woman who'd spoken to her.

'Fine!' Then, since from the woman's expression it was obvious that she hadn't done her usual good job of putting on a front, she said, 'Well, not that fine, actually. I've just stormed out in a strop but, since I've left my keys behind, I'm going to have to go back inside and get them.'

'Oh, bad luck! Men are just so smug when that happens.'

She hadn't mentioned a man, but the woman was offering her hand. 'I'm Amy Hallam. I live across the green. And you're Fleur Gilbert.'

'I am?' Then, 'Well, yes, I am. Have we met?'

Amy had all the elegance she'd imagined. Beautifully tailored linen trousers, a silk shirt, cashmere sweater. She also had four children. Three boys ranging from about six to ten years old, fooling around in her wake, and a little girl, a toddler, tucked on her hip. There were a couple of dogs, too. A springer spaniel, tangling one of the younger boys up in its lead, as well as a much better-behaved Labrador.

'You do look vaguely familiar,' Fleur added, and it was true. She did.

'Lots of people say that,' Amy said, 'but I'm afraid I'm cheating. Matt showed me a photograph of you.'

'Oh?' A photograph? 'It must have been an old one.'

'Not that old. It was of you at your graduation.'

Damn! Now she really was going to cry…

Someone, one of their witnesses, had taken photographs of them both on the steps of the register office after their wedding. She'd never seen them. No doubt whoever had taken them had decided that by the time they were processed neither bride nor groom would want to be reminded of the day and had stuffed them in the back of a drawer and forgotten about them.

Her graduation photograph was the last one she'd given him. He hadn't come to the ceremony because her parents were there—the last time she'd seen them together—but when the set of photographs had arrived she'd given him one of the small ones to keep in his wallet and, despite everything, he'd apparently hung on to it. Carried it with him.

Had showed it to a stranger on a plane.

Amy took an envelope out of the bag she had slung over her shoulder and said, 'I was just about to leave this with Matt. It's an invitation for your little boy to a bit of a do we're having for the village children on Easter Monday. Parents are welcome too, of course. I hope you'll both come.'

He'd showed this woman her picture, had talked about his son. What had he said?

'Matt's in the kitchen. If you want to give it to him.'

'It's so easy to walk off in a temper. Desperately hard to walk back. It helps to have a reason.' Amy held out the envelope to her and, as she took it, touched her arm briefly in a gesture of comfort, reassurance. Then, briskly, 'Don't dress Tom in anything good. Unless it's pouring with rain, they'll be outside for most of the time and if it's wet we'll be in the village hall. Whatever happens, they will get dirty.'

'Right.' Then, to her retreating back, 'Thank you.'

Amy, busy rounding up her boys, just raised a hand.

Fleur watched her for a moment as she laughed at something her smallest boy had said, kissing the baby girl tucked on her hip. There was something familiar about Amy Hallam, but that wasn't what held her attention. It was that she exuded contentment, an ease with life that she seemed to pass on with her touch.

When, finally, she turned away to look back to the cottage, she knew Matt would be standing in the doorway, waiting for her to crawl back. Submit to his terms.

She didn't crawl, she walked. It should have felt like capitulation, but it didn't. On the contrary. She owed it to Tom to hang in there, get it right this time, and that gave her more strength, not less.

'You came back,' he said, and indeed he did look ridiculously smug but, instead of making her angry, she just wanted to smile.

She didn't though. He wouldn't understand a smile. Instead, she stood in front of him and said, 'It's easy to run away, Matt. It takes courage to come back.' And this time she was the one who made the gesture, reached out, touched his arm, as Amy had touched hers.

She wasn't sure where that had come from, or what exactly she meant by it, but it seemed the right thing to do.

'You didn't have a choice. You forgot your car keys,' he said, pulling back as if her fingers had seared him through his sweater.

'And my tea,' she agreed, walking past him into the cottage, where she immediately set about pouring it into the two mugs. 'You, on the other hand, only forgot your manners.' She glanced back. He was standing in the kitchen door, watching her, forehead creased in a puzzled frown. 'I panicked when I got your letter, Matt. You intended that, I suppose.'

He didn't reply and, picking up both mugs, she waited for him to move so that she could return to the sitting room and the warmth of the fire.

CHAPTER SIX

FLEUR set the mugs on the hearth. Then, kneeling on the rug in front of the fire, she picked up the poker and stirred the embers.

'You were angry with me,' she said, not looking back to see if he'd followed her. Of course he'd followed her. She had what he wanted most in the world. 'And obviously it would be so much easier to get everything you wanted if I was frightened, off balance—'

'No.'

She glanced back at him, her expression letting him know that she wasn't buying it.

He shrugged. 'Okay, I was angry.'

Satisfied, she turned away. 'You say that as if I don't understand. Do you imagine that I didn't feel anger, too?' She poked at a log and it crumbled apart in a shower of sparks. 'I needed you, Matt, so much, and you just couldn't see it.' But then neither of them had been looking that hard. The tragedy, instead of pulling them closer together, had driven a barrier between them as high as any fence erected by their ancestors.

'I would have stood by you, but you were still too scared about what your father would think.'

'Did you really think that announcing we'd got secretly

married was going to help? My father had just learned, in the cruellest way, that his wife had been deceiving him. In what way would it have helped him to know that his daughter had been doing the same thing? When I agreed to a secret wedding you promised—'

'I promised that you would be the one to decide when to tell our families. But everything had changed.'

He joined her on the hearthrug, tossed a couple of logs on to the embers, held out his hand for the poker and took it, seemingly oblivious of the momentary touch of fingers. A touch that lanced through her, searing her to the bone.

'How could you have stayed?' he demanded, taking out his anger on the logs, jabbing at them, pushing them into the heart of the fire. He didn't say that he'd needed her. Probably he hadn't. He just couldn't take the fact that, faced with a crisis, forced to make a choice, she'd chosen duty over love.

Until then it had all seemed like a bit of a lark. Wonderfully wicked. Marriage had been the big mistake; neither of them had had the maturity to understand the consequences. Easy to see that later with the twenty-twenty vision of hindsight. With the short-sighted certainty and selfishness of youth, they'd thought that nothing could touch them. And Matt had been a golden youth.

At twenty-five he'd seemed to sail through life, effortlessly achieving everything he strived for. There had been nothing to touch his self-assurance, his certainty that life would be wonderful.

He'd always seemed so grown up, so much wiser than her, so sure of everything back then. He'd clearly fulfilled all that early promise, made a success of whatever he'd been doing for the last few years. But she'd been battling to keep her father from falling into a deep depression, to keep Gilbert

Fuchsias afloat, and five years of motherhood had given her a different kind of maturity. She was no longer a newly fledged graduate with the ink scarcely dry on her degree, let alone her marriage certificate.

'How could you have left?' He didn't answer and, at a disadvantage looking up at him from the hearthrug, she stood up. But even that felt suffocatingly close and she moved to the nearest armchair, settled on the arm. 'Why don't you stop playing games and tell me what you want?' she demanded.

'This isn't solitaire, Fleur.'

'It feels like it.' Correction, it had felt like it. She'd panicked when she'd got his letter, would have promised him anything—had promised him anything, as he'd been quick to remind her—if she could control what happened. But it occurred to her that she was already controlling the situation. She had something infinitely precious that he wanted and, unless he was prepared for a long and bitter court case, he needed her onside, her co-operation.

All he could do was threaten to tell the world that they were married. That Tom was his son. Well, they were going to have to do that anyway and he'd already shown himself willing to give her time to prepare Tom, prepare her father for the inevitable changes that would affect them all.

Then he'd spoiled it all by telling her he wanted something in return. Making it plain *what* he wanted in return for holding off until after Chelsea.

Looking at him, his arm thrown up against the high mantel, his forehead leaning against it as he stared down into the fire with the light of the flames licking around the logs throwing his face into sharp relief, touching his dark hair with gold, a tiny voice, an echo of the girl he'd left behind, whispered treacherously in her ear, 'Would that be so bad?' Tempting her with memories that stirred the dark longings that, no matter how deep she buried them, would never lie down and die, but bubble to the surface the minute she stopped concentrating.

She thought she'd wanted him to say the words out loud, to demonstrate just how far he'd strayed from the man she'd loved, making it easier to hate him.

Suddenly she didn't.

'You haven't got long, Matt,' she said abruptly. 'I have to pick up Tom at five.'

'You were talking to Amy,' he said, turning to look at her. 'What did she say to you?'

Not to run away. As if she sensed her inner turmoil, could read her mind. And, for a moment, her touch had given Fleur strength.

But it was easy to be strong standing outside, surrounded by the normality of spring flowers, other people's lives. Easy to be rational, sensible, when he wasn't looking at her as if… as if…

'She left an invitation for Tom,' she said, refusing to think about the way he was looking at her. 'For a party of some kind.' She took the envelope out of her pocket. 'On the holiday Monday after Easter.'

'That was thoughtful.' Then, 'Is it just for Tom?'

He wasn't crowding her. There was none of the overt sexual byplay that had precipitated her walk-out, yet as he straightened, reached for the invitation, she felt a hot prickle of awareness, an instant response to him that scared her witless.

Was that why she'd run? Fear that if he was really suggesting he'd make do with her as second best until she was ready to surrender his son to him, she wouldn't have the strength to tell him to go to hell.

'No!'

He stared at her, having no idea that she was not responding to his question but to what was in her head.

'No,' she repeated, rather less forcefully. 'Parents are invited, too.' On the point of handing the envelope to him, she thought better of it. Invitations to children—as Amy Hallam undoubtedly knew since she had so many of her own—went to their mother. She even managed a smile as she thumbed open the envelope, withdrew an invitation that had been handmade by a child. 'That's if you have a yearning to spend what will probably be one of Hanovers' busiest trading days of the year playing "pin the tail on the bunny" with a bunch of children.'

'It doesn't sound so bad.' For a moment his hand lingered within touching distance before he let it drop. 'I have, however, already made other plans for Easter.'

'Oh?' What kind of plans? 'I thought you were going to stay put until we'd sorted out custody arrangements for Tom?'

That brought a smile to his lips. 'Don't worry, Fleur. You're included.'

Don't worry? Was he kidding?

'I am?' she asked, hoping that she sounded a lot less bothered than she felt.

'Of course. I'm not letting you out of my sight until I've got everything I want. It's not that I'm concerned you'll run, you understand. We both know you're glued to your father's side. But you did promise me "anything" in return for the delay, time to prepare everyone for the truth, so here's the deal. Easter will be a family occasion this year. You, Tom and me, together at Disneyland in Paris.'

That was what happened, she thought, when you took your eye off the ball and started congratulating yourself on being the strong one. It bounced right back and whacked you in the eye.

And, for some reason, the fact that 'anything' turned out to be an innocent weekend in a theme park with Tom, rather than her in his bed, didn't improve things.

'Your father can come along as well, if he likes,' Matt said before she could voice her objection. 'That's entirely up to you. I'll bring my mother along and we'll make it a family party.'

'Oh, right. You're kidding…'

'Don't count on it. Just don't tell me that you can't leave him alone for a couple of days.'

As she'd been on the point of saying exactly that, it occurred to Fleur that Matt did seem to know a heck of lot about them. While her accusation that he'd been spying on them might have been overly neurotic, it was clear that he'd made good use of the time it had taken him to clear up his affairs, digging out information, not just about Tom, but about Gilberts. Presumably his enquiries had included what she'd been doing, too. He clearly knew all about her occasional trips to one of the caravans that their neighbour, Charlie Fletcher, kept on a site by the sea for renting out to holidaymakers. Not very exciting as holidays went, but since she only went in the off-season or when it wasn't wanted by paying customers Charlie was content to let her fill his window-boxes with her plants in lieu of rent. And Tom loved fishing with his net in the rock pools, building sandcastles, even if he did have to wrap up warm to do it.

It could hardly compete with a hug from Mickey Mouse though, or face-to-face encounters with pirates and princesses, or all the other wonderful fantasies Disney had to offer.

Tom, she thought, heart sinking, would be over the moon

with excitement at being taken on such a trip. Could she deny him that? Could she deny herself the joy of sharing it with him, of seeing Matt get to know his son?

'Or maybe it's a busy time for Gilberts, too?' he prompted. 'What?'

'The public holiday? Maybe you're rushed off your feet with people wanting to stuff their window-boxes and hanging baskets with your prize-winning fuchsias?'

She had the feeling that he was offering her a ready-made excuse, seeing if she'd lie to wriggle out of his invitation— no, make that his command.

'It's a long time since any of our fuchsias have won prizes,' she said. 'And I'd have thought that whoever's been snooping around on your behalf would have told you that we don't sell retail on site these days. Why would anyone come to us when your mother always chooses to sell fuchsias on a buy-one-get-one-free deal? Honey to bring in the punters who'll then spend a fortune on compost and fertiliser and fancy pots.'

'Sounds like good business to me.'

'Did I suggest that it was anything else?' Fleur enquired evenly, keeping her temper with difficulty.

'Not in so many words.' Then, 'I don't suppose you can afford to pay double to bring in packers over a public holiday.'

Irritated by his continuing emphasis on the contrast between Hanovers and Gilberts, she said, 'Whether I could or not, I wouldn't. Your mother isn't the only one who can work out what is likely to make money and what will certainly lose it.'

'In that case there's nothing to stand in your way. I'll send you an email with all the details.'

'Don't bother.'

There was a moment of unreal silence before he said, 'You're telling me that I have to give you what you want, but you give me nothing in return?' He paused, anticipating some response. When he didn't get it, he went on, 'It's not as if I'm demanding that you tell Tom I'm his father. I'm quite sure he's used to your boyfriend tagging along on holiday.'

'Excuse me?'

'Charlie Fletcher usually accompanies you on your trips to the sea, doesn't he?'

'Charlie?' While it was true that Charlie did sometimes turn up at the site when she was there, it was only to carry out maintenance and repairs on the other vans. That was what he did in the off season. And they did talk in the evenings, when Tom was asleep. At least Charlie had talked, about his wife, who'd died tragically young from a rare form of cancer. She'd mostly listened. 'Charlie is old enough to be my father,' she pointed out, refusing to lose her temper.

'Only if he was a sexually precocious fourteen-year-old.'

'I have no knowledge of his sex life at any age. He's a kind man, Matt. A friend.'

'I could be your…friend.'

Obviously she'd been a little quick to leap to her conclusion that the weekend would be innocent. She looked up at him, no longer staring into the flames but leaning against the mantel. A man relaxed, at ease, supremely confident of his power to get what he wanted.

She shook her head. No way. 'I'm sorry, Matt—' and she was sorry, sorrier than she could ever say '—but friends don't threaten you or attempt to browbeat you into doing something you know to be wrong.'

'Wrong?'

Maybe, on reflection, she thought, that had sounded a little priggish.

'I'm suggesting a little fun, that's all. What's wrong with that?'

Everything.

Was this how it was going to be from now on?

Was she going to become the dull parent, the enforcer, playing the heavy over homework and bedtimes, having to make the difficult decisions, use the word 'no,' while Matt waltzed in and out whenever it pleased him with exciting presents, holidays?

Did it actually matter, if it meant that Tom had even a small piece of his father?

Actually, she thought it did.

Her son deserved more than that. And, hard as it was to share him, she thought that Matt deserved more, too, which was why she was going to have to play the heavy with him.

'I'm going to have to ask you to put the fantasy holiday on hold for a while, Matt.'

'You'd rather we all spent the weekend in some dreary caravan?'

'It's not dreary, it's cosy and it's fun, but you don't actually have that option either. Charlie's vans are booked months in advance for the peak weeks by paying customers. But Disney is too much, too soon. You have to build up trust, do the small things first.' Seeing him frown, she tried again. 'You have to *earn* trips like that, Matt.'

'Earn them? How? With sleepless nights? Taking turns on the nappy rota? Playing at bathtime—'

'Matt…'

'Reading bedtime stories, perhaps?'

She wasn't fooled by his apparently mild query.

'Matt, please—'

'Don't "Matt" me!' Without warning, the poker clattered against the stone hearth as he gripped the back of the chair, pinning her between his arms, leaning in close so that his face was inches from hers. Startled, she backed away, until there was nowhere to go, but quickly realised that she'd misjudged him. It wasn't anger heating up his cool grey eyes, it was pain. 'You robbed me of all that, Fleur. Five years of the joy of watching my boy do everything for the first time. Of knowing him, loving him. If I took him away from you, took five years of his life from you—'

A cry of anguish escaped her lips. It happened, she knew it happened, and once a child had been whisked out of the country it might be years before he or she could be reunited with their mother.

If ever.

Eastern Europe was a big place. A place where he was at home, would have allies. And she would not.

'If I did that to you,' he ground out over her distress, 'you would still be ahead.' For a long moment he didn't move but kept her there, pinned to the back of the chair. 'And yet you'd still deny me a couple of days watching his face light up with excitement.' Then, as if recollecting himself, he straightened, stepped back, found a self-mocking little smile from somewhere and said, 'What exactly is your problem with that, Fleur? Are you scared I'll woo him away from you with treats and toys?'

She slumped down into the seat of the chair as if she'd been held against its back by some crushing forcefield that had suddenly dissipated. Swallowed. Finally managed a croaky, 'No.' Then she shook her head to emphasize the point. 'I'm not afraid of that. Tom deserves all the treats going. My fear is that you think that's all he needs.'

'Then you can relax. I'm in the process of setting up a trust fund. His education, his future, will be taken care of whatever happens to Gilberts.'

'That's not what I meant.'

'You want more? A fat divorce settlement, half my worldly goods in return for your co-operation?'

Divorce? Of course. He'd be going for the package deal. A man of his age, his stature, would want to clear the decks, sort his life so that he could look for a wife who would put him first—a woman who wasn't loaded down with the baggage of family history.

Maybe, she thought, he had someone picked out already.

'I don't want your money,' she said, doing her best to ignore her own feelings. She had no right to feel anything. Tom was her only concern now but, afraid that he would never understand, she lifted her hand in a gesture of despair. 'Our little boy has waited a long time for a father—'

'Damn it, Fleur…'

'—I don't want him confusing you with that guy in a red coat who drops in once a year on the twenty-fifth of December. What's his name?' She looked up and saw that Matt was scowling. 'Oh, yes. Father Christmas.'

Then, because she was actually feeling quite sick, she stood up, pushing past him, in need of fresh air.

'You can't go. We haven't settled anything,' he said, catching hold of her shoulders, stopping her. Forcing her to look at him. 'Or rather, I've given you what you wanted while I, as usual, get nothing.'

'Not true. I gave you everything.'

She'd given him her heart when she was eighteen years old and still at school. She'd given him her body not long after, and then her life and everything that went with it—sacrificing the biggest day in a woman's life for a five-minute ceremony in a register office because he'd said that once they were married they could never be parted.

'You threw it away in a fit of macho pride.'

And she shook herself free.

'Why don't you email me an agenda for our next meeting?' she suggested. 'Maybe that way you'll manage to stick to the point instead of getting personal.' She retrieved her bag from the sofa and headed for the door. 'In the meantime, I'll put Amy Hallam's party in Tom's diary.'

'Don't forget to put supper with Kay and Dom Ravenscar in yours,' he reminded her. 'Friday, seven-thirty for eight.'

'Don't push your luck, Matt.'

'Don't push yours, Fleur.'

'Fleur!'

She watched Tom run all the way into school, not wanting to miss any of the precious moments while he was still entirely hers. Soon enough her world would disintegrate and she'd join the ranks of parents with empty weekends, whole empty weeks in the holidays to fill.

Only when he'd disappeared from view did she turn to acknowledge Sarah's shout, waiting while she caught up and let her own two loose in the school yard.

'Nearly late again. I need to lose weight,' she said, turning to Fleur.

'Come and spend next week packing for me,' she suggested, not particularly eager to get home and confront the problem of the overdraft, or the surveyor arriving at nine-thirty. 'A few days working under glass will do more for you than a week at a health farm. And it won't cost you a penny.'

'I should hope not. In fact I'm pretty sure that the way it works is that you have to pay me,' Sarah added with a grin.

'This is a new scheme I've come up with where I market it as an alternative holiday. Did you know that there are people who actually pay to spend their holidays on blighted moors rebuilding drystone walls and repairing footpaths?'

'I had heard. Conservation holidays, they're called. I don't think you come under the same heading.'

'Perhaps not, but I wouldn't charge them for the privilege. Just think about it. They'd learn all about plant production during the day, having plenty of exercise in a sauna like atmosphere and then in the evening there's all that traditional village nightlife—'

'I assume you're referring to shove-ha'penny at the King's Head?'

'—and, as a bonus, they could camp in a historic barn with resident barn owl. Who could resist?'

'I've thought about it and I'll pass,' Sarah said with a grin. Then, 'How's your dad? When I called the other evening to speak to you, he sounded a bit low, I thought.'

'Dad?' Fleur felt the colour drain from her face. 'The other evening?' she asked. 'What evening?'

'Monday? Yes, it must have been Monday. Didn't he tell you I'd called?'

No, he hadn't told her. If he'd told her, he'd have had to confront the fact that she'd lied to him. Deal with it. He never had been prepared to do that, she thought. He'd just buried his head in the sand. It was why they were in such a mess financially. If he'd once taken the slightest interest in anything her mother did. If he'd ever once said, No…

'I wanted to finalise the details of the Easter egg hunt with you, but he said you'd gone out.' Sarah waited, clearly hoping for details, but when Fleur didn't respond she went on, 'Well, that was the excuse. I just wanted a bit of gossip, to be honest. Have you heard that Matthew Hanover is home? There's a lot of speculation on the reason for his return and everyone wants to know if he's going to stay.'

'Why would you think I'd know?' She looked at Sarah, searching her face for some deeper meaning. Did she know? Suspect the truth?

'Hey! No reason. Good grief, I didn't think you were so touchy about that old feud.'

'I'm not. I'd be happy to forget the whole thing.' She raised a hand as if to dismiss it. 'Tell me the gossip.'

'Well, there's nothing, to be honest, just speculation. You know how nature abhors a vacuum.'

'I had heard a rumour to that effect.'

Sarah grinned, then said, 'I saw him driving through the village yesterday in the slinkiest black sports car you could imagine. Dark hair, rock-like profile.' She flapped her hand in front of her face in a cooling gesture. 'Why is it that while women sag, men improve with age?'

'They need us more than we need them. They have to keep us interested.'

'I could be deeply interested,' Sarah replied.

'Sarah Carter, you're a respectable married woman.'

'I'm married,' she said. 'Isn't that enough? Do I have to be respectable as well?' Then, realising that she hadn't been exactly tactful, 'Sorry. But honestly, the man is going to set local hearts aflutter.'

'He always did,' Fleur said distractedly. All she could think about was how quiet her father had been in the last couple of days. He was never exactly talkative and she'd been too pre-occupied with her own worries to notice how withdrawn he'd been, barely answering her when she spoke.

Now she knew why.

She should have told him. The minute she'd read Matt's letter she should have gone home, told him everything. Instead she'd tried to protect him, shield him for a few more weeks.

Stupid, stupid…

'Hey, where are you off to? Can't I tempt you to a cup of coffee, a slice of chocolate cake?'

'I have to get home, Sarah,' she said, already on the move. 'There's something I need to do.' And, without stopping to explain, she started to run.

CHAPTER SEVEN

FLEUR found her father lying on the floor of his glasshouse, a plant pot beside him, compost scattered in a long arc extending from his arm, where it had been flung out as he'd fallen.

He wasn't unconscious, but he couldn't get up.

He tried to speak, but the words made no sense.

A stroke, she thought, as she jabbed the emergency number into her mobile. She'd done a first aid course and knew there was a golden hour. If he had treatment within the hour the effects would be minimised, a full recovery possible.

How long had he been lying there?

It couldn't be more than twenty minutes. She'd spoken to him just before she'd left the house. He'd scarcely looked up, but he'd been fit enough to walk from the kitchen, start work on the tedious daily job of giving each of his plants a quarter turn to ensure that it grew straight and true.

'Hush, Dad,' she said. 'I'm here. It's going to be all right. I'm going to put you in the recovery position,' she said, and when that was done she stripped off her coat and covered him. 'The ambulance is on the way. Good job you didn't keel over in the kitchen. It's much warmer in here,' she said, talking non-stop, wanting him to know that she was there. That she wouldn't leave him.

He tried to say something. She didn't need to understand the words to know he was saying that the plants were more important.

She wanted to tell him not to talk such rubbish, but there was something much more important she had to say and, curling up beside him on the floor, her arms around him, holding him, she said, over and over, 'I'm sorry, Dad. No more lies... No more lies...'

'No more lies,' she whispered again, pressing her cheek against his—not sure whether it was his cheek that was wet or her own—before surrendering him to the medics, answering their questions, watching as they checked for vital signs and inserted a line in his arm, feeling utterly helpless.

'Fleur?'

She spun around at the sound of Matt's voice. On the floor her father began to struggle, tried to speak.

'Go away. Leave. Can't you see how you're upsetting him?'

'I saw the ambulance as I drove into the village. When it stopped here...'

He'd thought it was Tom, she realised and, without thinking, she reached out to touch his arm, reassure him that she understood.

'Is it his heart?'

'A stroke, I think.' Then, realising what she was doing, she snatched her hand away. 'Happy now?' she asked, and was glad to see him blench. And then, finally working out what her father was trying to say, 'For goodness' sake, you idiot, shut the door before you wipe out a year's work!'

She meant him to shut it on the way out but, although

he closed the door, he remained on the inside and she was, despite everything, glad of his presence. And when he moved nearer, took her hand and held it as they stood in silence while the medics went about their work, she didn't pull away.

Finally, when they'd got him on to the gurney, one of the medics said, 'We're ready to go now, Miss. Are you coming in the ambulance with your dad, or do you want to follow us in your own car?'

'I'll come in the ambulance,' she said, relinquishing the guilty comfort of Matt's hand.

'I'll follow you,' he said. 'You'll need a lift home.'

'I managed to get home for six years without you, Matt. I can manage this.' Then she pushed past him, not looking back as she followed her father to the waiting ambulance.

Matt had done as she'd asked once before when she'd told him to stay away. His mistake, and one he wasn't about to repeat. But before he followed he picked up the spilled plant, settled it back in its pot and set it on the staging. Then he made sure all the glasshouses were secure before going to the house and doing the same with that.

It was just as well he did.

The back door was unlocked and he went inside, checked that there was nothing left simmering on the stove, that the fire was safe in the living room.

The dog looked up from her basket, but if she was supposed to protect the family home she fell down miserably on the job, allowing him to rub her behind the ear before letting her nose drop back on her paws.

Then, having made certain that everything was secure, he took the key out of the back door, locked up and walked back to his car, planning to drive out to the hospital and wait for Fleur, no matter how long it took.

As he rounded the side of the house, a man standing by the front door—having clearly just rung the doorbell—looked up from the clipboard he was holding.

'Mr Gilbert?' And when Matt neither confirmed nor denied his identity, he went on, 'Derek Martin, Martin and Lord, Surveyors. I'm here to do a valuation. For the bank?'

That, he thought, didn't sound good.

'Now?' he asked.

'Miss Gilbert is expecting me at nine-thirty.' He glanced at his watch. 'I may be a minute or two early.'

'You have some identification? A letter of instruction?'

He produced them and, having checked them, Matt said, 'Miss Gilbert has been called away on a family emergency. Do you have to see the inside of the house?'

'Just a quick look round to check the scope of the accommodation, look out for anything structural. Anyone buying at this end of the market is likely to want to gut the place and start again.'

'Give me a moment while I call her and ask what she wants me to do,' Matt said, walking out of earshot and calling Fleur's mobile. She must have already reached the hospital because he was only getting her voice mail. Since putting the man off, and alerting the bank to more trouble, was not going to help Fleur, he made the decision to go ahead anyway and left a message letting her know that he was taking care of it. One thing less for her to worry about.

Maybe.

His mother had been right about one thing, he decided, as he escorted Martin through the house. It would make a lovely family home, if you had the family to fill it. Three or four children minimum, with a dog apiece to add the kind of giddy mayhem which, as an only child, he'd envied in other people's houses when he'd been a boy.

The kitchen was large, with the kind of shabby comfort that made him feel right at home, but he only had eyes for a huge old refrigerator festooned with crayon pictures drawn by Tom and photographs of him at all ages. It was all he could do to resist taking one, slipping it into his pocket.

The living room, probably once a breakfast room, needed pale walls and French windows opening out on to the garden.

The office was functional, neat, the computer hardware, like everything else, in need of upgrading.

With a proper family in residence the huge drawing room and the long panelled dining room, where presumably Fleur's grandparents had once thrown those great parties, could be opened up, the dust-sheets removed, fires lit to fill the huge grates and send warmth and light flickering over the polished surfaces.

Right now they were simply cold and empty.

He followed Derek Martin upstairs but remained on the broad landing, staring out of the window, while the man stuck his head around the door of each room.

'That's impressive.'

He turned to see what had caught the man's attention.

'On the door of the kid's room,' Martin said. 'A family tree going back to the early nineteenth century.'

'That's when the Gilberts settled on this land and built the original part of the house,' Matt told him, going closer to look at the beautifully drawn family tree on which the last entry was the birth of his son: Fleur's work, he'd know her handwriting anywhere. Only the mother's line was shown, of course. The paternal side was missing. Maybe he should draw the matching half and give it to Tom, help him line it up so that he could see for himself how the families were joined by his parents, Fleur Gilbert and Matthew Hanover, with his own name, right in the centre at the bottom, cementing the two halves together.

Thomas Gilbert Hanover.

'Are you done in the house?' he asked, turning away.

'Just about. I've got the dimensions of the land from an earlier survey, but I'll need to check the buildings. There's a barn?'

'It's right at the bottom of the field, on the boundary line.'

That had been something else for the two families to fall out over. The Gilberts had gotten the barn, the Hanovers had a little more land, and each generation had argued over who'd got the best of the deal.

'I can manage if you've got to be somewhere else,' Derek Martin said, apparently picking up on Matt's impatience to be out of the house.

But there was nothing he could do at the hospital for the moment except, in all likelihood, agitate Fleur. Maybe in an hour or so she'd be so glad to see someone, anyone, that she wouldn't care who it was. In the meantime he'd be more useful here, making sure the surveyor didn't leave any glasshouse doors open.

'How is he?'

'Comfortable.' The doctor smiled. 'Luckily we were able to get the clot-busting drugs into him quickly and while it'll take time, some intensive physio and speech therapy, your father should make a good recovery, Miss Gilbert.'

'How long will he have to stay in hospital?'

He hated hospitals. She hated hospitals...

'Let's see how it goes, shall we? As soon as there's a bed available he'll be moved up to the ward, but in the meantime you can stay with him if you like. Or maybe you'd rather go home and fetch him the things he'll need?'

'I want to see him first.'

She had things to say. Promises to make.

'Dad?' She pushed open the treatment room door. He was propped up on a trolley, a tube inserted into his chest. His eyes were closed but he seemed to be breathing easily and the machines monitoring his vital signs were bleeping steadily, reassuringly.

She picked up a chair and moved it so that she could sit beside him, taking his hand, holding it in hers and, after a moment, he squeezed it, acknowledging her presence.

This was it. He already thought the worst he could of her and she had to live with what that knowledge had done to him. All she had left was the truth.

'Matt Hanover…' she began. 'Matt is Tom's father, Dad.'

The machines skittered for a second or two before settling back into a steady rhythm. Then her father tried to speak, struggling with words that wouldn't come out the way he wanted them to. But eventually she worked out what he was trying to ask her.

'Did I love him?'

That was all he cared about?

'Yes,' she said. 'I loved him.'

She didn't know the words to express the way she'd loved Matthew Hanover. There had never been anyone else since she had first caught sight of him through a gap in the fence. There never would be anyone else.

Outside in the corridor nurses and doctors went about their business, in the waiting room a child cried plaintively, but no one disturbed them as Fleur recounted every moment of her forbidden love, the years of worshipping Matt as a distant, unreachable, god-like figure, daydreaming about him, timing her arrival home from school to coincide with his. Never speaking, always on the opposite side of the road, the other side of the fence. But always aware of him. Always certain that he was aware of her.

She looked at her father. His eyes were closed again and she was no longer sure that he could hear her, but she went on anyway, smiling a little as she confessed that her good grades at school had been purely down to Matt. By the time she'd been working on her A-levels he'd been away at university and she'd just wanted to stay at home and work, knowing that while she was at her desk she wouldn't miss a single chance glimpse of him from her bedroom window on his rare visits home.

'Stupid,' she said.

Seth Gilbert tightened his grip on her hand, mumbled something. *Not stupid...*

Reassured, she told him how, invited to a twenty-first birthday party being thrown for one of her classmates' older brothers, she'd finally come face to face with him for the first time.

Her father managed a lopsided smile.

'Romeo and Juliet?' she translated.

Again he squeezed her hand.

'Yes, Dad,' she whispered, through a throat suddenly thick and painful with held back tears. 'We thought we were Romeo and Juliet. Right down to the secret wedding.'

How wrong could she have been?

* * *

Outside in the corridor Matt, held captive with his hand against the door, didn't move, knowing how important this was, not for him, but for Fleur. She needed to unburden herself, seek her father's forgiveness, purge herself of years of bottled-up guilt.

He hadn't understood that. How guilty she'd felt. He'd been too angry, too busy wallowing in his own sense of grievance, to see what she had been going through, to reassure her that it wasn't her fault. That she had nothing to feel guilty about.

He'd behaved with all the maturity of a baby throwing its teddy from a pram.

Even when his own tears spilled over and ran down his cheeks and he wanted to go to her, beg her to forgive him, he held his silence, raising a hand to stop a nurse from bursting in and disturbing them. Words were too easy. Forgiveness had to be earned, paid for with deeds—as she'd paid over the years with hard work, caring.

'Oh, listen to me,' he heard her say with a telltale sniff. He didn't need to see her to know that she was searching her pockets for a tissue. She blew her nose. 'Sitting here gabbing when I should be going home to fetch your pyjamas, a toothbrush.' He heard her chair move as she stood up. 'You'll be fine, Dad, don't you worry. You'll be back on your feet in no time.'

He heard Seth Gilbert struggle to speak. Then Fleur said, 'It's okay. Don't worry about a thing. I'll manage.'

Matt let his hand fall, stepped back so that the nurse could get on with her job, then turned and walked swiftly back to the main entrance so that Fleur wouldn't know he'd been listening to her spill her heart out.

He was waiting outside the main entrance when she finally

appeared, phone to her ear as she checked her messages. Heard her muttered expletive. That would be his, he guessed, and he said, 'Problem?'

She jumped, physically jumped, at the sound of his voice. Her nose was a little pink, her eyes a touch watery, but they still flashed as she said, 'I told you not to come.'

'You did. I've learned from my mistake. Maybe you should, too.'

She caught her breath as if to deny making any mistake other than listening to him, but she clearly thought better of it and instead gestured with the phone.

'Did the surveyor say when he's coming back?'

'No need. I had the back door key so I let him in.'

'You did *what?*'

'Your back door was open. I checked that everything was safe and then locked up. I was going to bring you the key.'

'But instead you decided to go ahead and give Derek Martin the guided tour. Well, you were complaining that you hadn't ever been inside the house. You can tick that one off your list of complaints.'

'I wasn't complaining, I was making a point,' he said. 'And you never came in my home either.'

'I never wanted to.'

'Really? You weren't the teeniest bit curious? Didn't once wonder what it would be like to make out there while my parents were out?'

She blushed, lifted one shoulder about half an inch.

He just about managed to keep a straight face.

'The surveyor didn't stay long,' he said as if he hadn't noticed. 'He was just going through the motions if you want my opinion—'

'Which I don't.' Then, trying very hard not to look anxious, 'What did he say?'

'Nothing much. He was more interested in the basic structure, assuming that whoever bought the house would want to gut it and start again from scratch.' He made no attempt to sweeten the pill, despite the fact that, despite all attempts to give as good as she got, she was clearly sagging, looking for all the world like a rag doll with the stuffing knocked out of her. 'And that the land was perfect for a "nice little housing development."'

'On a cold day in hell.'

'He was also of the opinion that the barn would be "snapped up" by some city dweller looking for a country home.'

'Dream on.'

'He got quite excited about it. Said he knew someone who'd pay a premium for that kind of property.'

'He clearly doesn't know about your mother.'

'My mother might be able to scare off a local builder, but someone with serious intent and a good architect wouldn't have any problem getting a conversion through on appeal. Especially if the major objector could be shown to be less than objective, having plans of her own for the place.'

'You wouldn't do that to your own mother!'

'Maybe not, but I'm sure you could. Give the man a call.'

'Maybe I will.'

He nodded. 'In the meantime his valuation should reflect the development possibilities of the site, which will at least give you some breathing space.' Then, 'How's your father doing?'

'My father is doing just fine, no thanks to either of us, but I don't have time to chat; I have to get home and pick up things for him.' She pressed the quick dial on her phone, but before she could lift it to her ear, he caught her wrist, took the phone, turned it off and put it in his pocket.

'Excuse me!'

'My car's this way,' he said, taking her arm.

'You can keep your car,' she said, digging her heels in. 'And I'll have my phone back, thank you very much.'

'Don't let's fight about it. Charlie Fletcher is ten miles away, while I'm here and ready to take you home.'

'Still telling me how it's going to be, Matt?'

'You know it makes sense.'

She looked up at him and he saw the faintest glimmer of something that might have been the prelude to a smile lighting her eyes. Not one of those forced, slightly desperate smiles she had used to face him down, attempting to convince him that she wasn't going down without a fight, but the real thing. It reminded him so much of the girl he'd fallen in love with at first sight, first touch, at the first scent of her hair as she'd laid her head against his shoulder, lost his heart to with one sweet kiss, that for a moment he couldn't breathe.

It would be so easy to fall in love with her all over again, he thought. Except, of course, he'd never fallen out of love with her.

He'd done his best to blot out his feelings, burying them under a heap of pride and anger, fury that his plan, his life, had been so thoroughly messed up by two selfish adults who hadn't cared who got hurt in the crossfire of their passion.

A selfishness he'd compounded, nurturing his own petty grievances, choosing to believe that he was the brave one, walking away, venturing out on his own, telling himself that she was pathetic, weak, afraid.

He'd been wrong about that. Wrong about a lot of things. She'd done what she had to do without complaint.

He should have stayed and helped her. Supported his mother through her own bad times.

He'd blamed Fleur because he'd missed five years of his son's life but it wasn't her fault. He'd got his just deserts and he recognised the truth in what she'd said, that he had to earn his place in all their lives, not with grand gestures, fantasy holidays, but by being there.

'For your information, not that it's any of your business, I wasn't going to call Charlie. I was going to call Sarah Carter. She could have done double duty,' she explained.

He resisted the urge to tell her that it damn well was his business. That he was making it his business. He had years of doing anything but make her life his business to make up for. So he contented himself with, 'I can do two things at once.'

'I don't doubt it, but I can't quite see you casually posting a gossip bulletin at the village store as you stock up on the basics. Everyone will have seen the ambulance and will want to know the details. It will be a kindness to put them out of their misery.'

'Do they deserve your kindness?'

She shrugged. 'One earns Brownie points where one can,' she said, 'and I suspect, once the big news story breaks, I'm going to need all I can get.'

'If anyone says a word out of place, tell me and they'll wish they hadn't,' he assured her. Then, having got her full attention, he went on, 'And you can ring Sarah and give her all the details while I drive you home. That way she'll be able to start spreading the news even more quickly.'

'That's true.'

Finally, she'd agreed with one thing he'd said. Making the most of it, he continued, 'And, since I'm here, it does seem a scandalous waste of valuable resources to have her drive all the way here and back.'

'Scandalous,' she agreed a touch breathlessly, and this time he met no resistance as he took Fleur's elbow in his hand and eased her in the direction of his car.

'Then,' he said, 'while you're putting things together for your dad, I'm just as capable as Sarah Carter of making you a nice of cup of tea with plenty of sugar.' He bent to open the door. 'For the shock.'

She snorted. He suspected, hoped, it was with laughter.

'You,' she said, sliding on to the low seat, 'are no Sarah.' Then, holding out her hand, 'Telephone?'

He returned her mobile phone without comment and she was already talking by the time he pulled out of the car park.

She spent the journey not just calling Sarah, but rounding up some of her part-time staff to come in and cover for her. She was going to need more help than that, he thought.

He wondered if she realised just how much.

Seth Gilbert was going to need a lot of care when he was released from hospital. Who knew how long it would be before he was fit enough to look after himself?

Even if he made a miraculous recovery, there was no way he was going to be able to do anything to help with the huge task of preparing for a premier show such as Chelsea.

That was a full-time job.

He considered mentioning it to Fleur, but in the end decided that she had enough to worry about for the moment. Besides, he was rapidly catching on to the fact that actions spoke louder than words.

CHAPTER EIGHT

WHILE Fleur was upstairs sorting out the things her father would need, Matt put together a sandwich and made a pot of tea. When she appeared in the doorway, ready to dash back to the hospital without pausing for breath, he held out a kitchen chair, determined that she would go nowhere until she'd at least taken a mouthful of food.

'Oh,' she said, clearly taken aback. 'You shouldn't have. I don't have time…' She hovered, clearly desperate to fly back to the hospital, but unwilling to appear ungrateful. 'I'll put it in the fridge and have it when I can get back,' she said.

Pretty much what he'd anticipated, in fact.

'I don't think that's a good idea.'

'Matt…'

'You'll be no use to anyone if you run yourself into the ground. Your dad and Tom need you to be there for them.' He shoved back the wicked thought that if she collapsed she'd be forced to stop pushing him away, would have to admit that she couldn't manage without him.

It wasn't true. She'd had to manage without him.

He'd run when he should have stayed. Now he had to be patient, be there, fill the need, before she recognised it herself. She'd told him that he had to earn his place in Tom's life.

Once he'd taken her love for granted, as his right. He'd tossed that away and now he had to earn his place in her life, too, if they were ever to be a family. And that was what he wanted, he realised, more than anything. Not to divide out Tom's life in parcels between them, but to be together, always.

He continued to wait and, after a moment, she dropped the bag she was holding and sank into the chair. 'Who is picking up Tom from school?' he asked, pouring out a single cup of tea, piling in the sugar.

'I don't take sugar.'

'You won't even notice it,' he assured her. 'Tom?' he prompted.

'Sarah offered. She's going to take him home, give him tea, take care of him until I can pick him up,' she said quickly, before he could volunteer.

She needn't have worried. There was nothing he wanted more than to be close to his son, but at the moment they were strangers. With his grandfather in hospital the child would need to be with someone he knew, felt safe with.

One step at a time.

'Is there anything you need?' he asked. 'Anything I can do? You'll be all right driving back to the hospital? If you're still shaky—'

'No.' Then, 'No, really, thank you, Matt. You've done more than enough.'

Actually, he hadn't even started, but he didn't say that. He just said, 'In that case, if you'll promise you'll finish your sandwich, I'll get out of your way.'

He caught her momentary look of surprise, disappointment—or maybe he just wanted to believe that was what he saw—before she nodded. 'Of course. You must have a million things to do.'

'Not a million,' he said. 'Nothing that won't keep if you need me.'

'No. Really.'

She was very firm. Very determined, he thought.

Then she made a brave stab at a smile. 'I'm sorry if I seemed less than grateful earlier. You've really been an enormous help.'

He allowed himself the luxury of letting his hand rest briefly on her shoulder before he said, 'You have my mobile number. Call me if I you need anything. Day or night.' He didn't need to spell it out. 'Night' would be bad news. 'And don't forget to ring Derek Martin, too.' He picked up his jacket and headed for the door. 'Let him know you're interested in serious offers for the barn.'

'Don't you care about your mother's plans?' she asked.

Not as much as I care about yours...

'If she wants your barn badly enough, she'll pay the market price,' he said. 'And be polite about it.'

Fleur didn't rush to finish her sandwich. She took her time, drank the tea—and Matt was right, it was wonderful.

She should be making plans, sorting out work rotas, doing a hundred and one different things, but somehow all she could think about was that brief touch of Matt's hand on her shoulder.

When she'd turned and seen him standing in the doorway of the glasshouse it had been all she could do not to throw herself into his arms. She'd so badly needed him to hold her, had needed him to tell her that it would be all right, just as she had all those years ago when her mother was dying, her father in a state of collapse.

He hadn't been there for her then and this time she'd

just shouted at him. Had told him to go away. Had learned nothing.

While he, it appeared, was finally listening. The only reason he'd stuck around this time was because he wanted to know what was happening. Because he wanted his son.

'Matt!' His mother looked up from her desk. 'I'd given you up for the day.'

'I'm sorry. I didn't realise I was expected to keep office hours.'

She laughed nervously, 'Of course not. You can come and go as you please. I just—'

'What's this?' he asked, cutting her short and holding up the copy of a letter that he'd spotted lying on the top of the filing tray in the outer office while his mother's secretary had been sorting out the list of messages she had for him.

She glanced at it and he was pleased to see that she coloured slightly. 'Nothing. Just Parish Council business.'

'Threatening Seth Gilbert with a fine if he doesn't cut his hedges? Is that the way things are done in Longbourne these days?'

'It's overgrown. A traffic hazard. It was discussed at last week's meeting and it was decided that a letter was the appropriate action.'

'A threatening letter?'

'You know nothing about it,' she said, standing up. 'Seth Gilbert has to be shown that he can't ignore the by-laws—'

'For your information, Seth Gilbert had a stroke this morning and he's in hospital.'

She rapidly lost the colour from her cheeks and for a moment her mouth worked as if she couldn't get out the words, but she finally managed it.

'It makes no difference.'

Disgusted, he tossed the letter on her desk, walked out of the office and down on to the sales floor, where he picked up a petrol-driven hedge-trimmer, a pair of safety goggles and gloves, cutting short the check-out girl when she began twittering about staff discount. He wasn't staff. He didn't want a discount. He just wanted to get out of there.

He could have picked up a telephone, organised someone to do the work for him. For Fleur.

Not good enough. He wanted his mother to see him do it himself. Wanted everyone to see.

Katherine Hanover watched him from her office window. 'You don't understand, Matt,' she said as if he was in the room, as if he could hear her. 'Seth has to learn. He has to pay…'

'Did you say something, Mrs Hanover?'

She turned to see Lucy, her secretary, standing in the doorway, eyeing her curiously.

'What? Oh, no, I was just, um, thinking out loud.'

Lucy didn't move. 'Is something wrong? Can I get you anything?'

'Wrong?'

Something tickled her cheek, but when she brushed it her fingers came away wet. For a moment she couldn't think why, then realised with a shock that tears were pouring down her face.

It was so long since she'd cried that she'd forgotten how it felt. She hadn't shed a tear when Phillip died. She should have done, she knew, and had felt so guilty, even though he'd been with Jennifer. He had been her husband for a long time; he was the father of her son. He'd been trapped and unhappy, too, and had deserved a few tears for that alone. She just hadn't been able to manage it.

She hadn't cried when Matt left either. Easy to see in hindsight that, a constant reminder of her mistakes, she'd deliberately driven him away. Well, she'd paid for that with long empty years, but he was home now so that was all right and her business was growing faster than she would have believed possible.

These days she was treated with serious respect. She had no need of tears.

'No, Lucy,' she said, lifting her head, 'there's nothing wrong.'

Her life was perfect. Just perfect…

'Why are you cutting my hedge?'

'If this is your hedge, you must be Tom Gilbert.' Matt had seen Tom from a distance, walking towards him with Sarah Carter and her two children, but he hadn't stopped work or done anything to suggest that he was waiting for them to draw level with him. If Tom hadn't spoken he'd have carried on with what he was doing.

But now he straightened, eased his back, pushing up the safety goggles. It had been a long time since he'd worked with his back bent, arms at full stretch, as his muscles were quick to remind him. Nor had he anticipated his first meeting with his son would be when he was sweaty, aching, with bits of hedge sticking to his hair and clothes. But maybe it was better this way, less forced or awkward and, hunkering down so that he was on the same level as the boy, he offered his hand.

'I'm Matt Hanover,' he said, half expecting the child to run screaming at the sound of his name.

He didn't. He just looked up at Sarah Carter, who nodded

and, reassured, Tom put out his own small hand and said, 'I'm Tom Gilbert.'

Letting go was about the hardest thing he'd ever done. He wanted to hoist the boy up into his arms, hug him, hold on to him. But he didn't do any of those things. He made do with the oddly formal little handshake and said, 'I'm delighted to meet you, Tom Gilbert, and, to answer your question, I'm cutting the hedge so that people driving through the village will have a clear view of the road.'

'Mum said it needed doing. She had a letter about it and she said a word I'm not allowed to say.' He leaned forward and whispered, confidentially, in his ear, 'It begins with a D.' He gave the letter its sound rather than its name.

'Right,' Matt said, torn between the desire to laugh and cry, both of them with sheer joy. 'Well, son, when you see her you can tell her that she doesn't have to worry about it any more.'

'Okay.'

Matt stood up before he lost it completely, nodding to Sarah. 'It's been a while, Sarah. How are you?'

'Good, thanks.' She introduced her own two children and then encouraged all three of them to climb over the stile and run on ahead along the footpath.

He frowned. 'Tell me, does your sister work at Hanovers?'

'No, she's working in London. It's my cousin Lucy who works for your mother, but we're very alike.' She added, 'It caused a bit of confusion when I did some temporary work on the tills during the Christmas rush.'

'I'm sure it did.' He had the feeling she was trying to tell him something.

'Come on, Sarah, I'm hungry,' Tom, lingering on the top of the stile, called. 'We're having sp'getti,' he confided to Matt.

'Lucky you,' he said.

'You're welcome to join us,' Sarah said.

Her invitation was tempting, but it would be cheating. He'd agreed with Fleur that she should set the timetable for getting to know Tom. Even this chance encounter was probably breaking her rules.

'Thanks, but it's going to take me a while to clear up the debris.' Then, 'Do you live at this end of the village now?'

'No. We're just taking the scenic route home along the footpath. Fleur told me she'd seen some bluebells.'

'They're further on, nearer the barn.' Because she didn't move on, he continued, 'So, tell me, does your cousin enjoy working for my mother?'

'She's a good boss. She rewards initiative, hard work. She invited us all up to her office for a drink when she closed on Christmas Eve, even the temps.'

'Well, good.'

'Did you know that she has a photograph of you on her desk? One of those school portraits. You must have been about six or seven years old. You had a tooth missing.'

'It's not there now. Maybe she thought it would embarrass me.'

'Maybe she doesn't need it now you're home. I hadn't realised you had such curly hair when you were young.'

'Bane of my life,' he said, running his hand over his head as if to smooth it, despite the fact that the curls had long ago been tamed by good cutting.

'It was a bit of a light bulb moment for me.'

And they both watched as Tom, distracted by the sight of a cock pheasant strutting along the hedgerow, made exactly the same gesture to flatten his hair.

'Come on, children, let's find these bluebells,' she said,

nodding to Matt, as she heaved herself over the stile. 'Say goodbye to Mr Hanover, children. Tom.'

'G'bye,' he said, then turned and ran off down the path.

'Sarah,' Matt called. 'Thank you.'

She didn't stop or look back, just raised a hand to acknowledge that she'd heard.

It took him the rest of the afternoon to finish the job and shift the debris, but by the time he left Fleur still hadn't arrived home.

It was late when she finally called him, but that was okay. He'd had plenty to do to keep him occupied, finally sinking into a hot bath to soak away aches that the quick shower had done nothing to ease when he'd gotten home.

When the phone finally rang he reached out, took it from the stool beside the bath, glanced at the caller ID and said, 'Fleur? Is there a problem?'

'No.' Then, 'No, everything's fine, thank you. Oh, Lord, is that the time? I hadn't realised how late it is. Have I disturbed you?'

Disturbed him? She'd disturbed him from the moment he'd first set eyes on her—a red-haired, green-eyed pixie peering through the fence, pulling faces at him until she'd been hauled away by her mother.

'If you really want to know, I'm up to my neck in hot water, soaking the pain from my aching limbs.'

'Oh.'

He heard her swallow, felt an answering thump from his own heart.

'Did you need something?' he asked.

'Oh, no. I just wanted to say thank you. Sarah told me what you did. And for clearing up the mess in the glasshouse too.'

'Just earning my dues,' he said. Not true. He hadn't even thought about Tom when he'd repotted the plant and cut the hedge. Only about Fleur. 'How's your father?' he asked.

'Fretting about his plants.' Then, 'Matt, about this morning…'

She paused, taking a breath, and he didn't need her to use her telephone to take a snapshot, send it to him, to fill in the picture. She'd be sitting at the kitchen table, legs twisted around each other, pushing a loose strand of hair behind her ear as she hunted for the right words…

'This morning?' he prompted.

'I think, in the heat of the moment, I might have blamed you for what happened. Something Sarah said after I dropped Tom off at school made me realise that Dad must have known I'd lied to him on Monday. About where I was going. When I met you. He'd been acting a bit off with me—'

'Then I'd suggest that what you were actually doing was attempting to offload your own feelings of guilt.'

'Yes,' she agreed, surprising him. 'You're absolutely right. The blame was entirely mine.'

'You do know a stroke isn't something brought on by a single shock, don't you, Fleur? He'll have been having symptoms for weeks. Headaches, trouble with his vision, confusion, numbness?' She didn't answer. 'Am I right?'

'Apparently. He kept it all to himself, of course. Didn't want me worrying about him.'

'That's the way parents are.'

'How do you know so much about it?'

'Parenthood?' he asked, unable to resist teasing her a little. She sounded so low.

'Strokes.'

'Oh, right. My grandmother had several. You know, your

dad probably had small incidents before. The kind of thing you just shake off, choose not to think about.'

'That's what the doctor said. Anyway, I wanted to apologise.'

'No need. I understood your need to lash out. No one better.'

For a moment neither of them spoke, but it wasn't an awkward silence. They used to do that when they couldn't meet for weeks at a time. Just call one another, listen to each other breathing. How he'd missed that closeness, that intimacy, that ability to communicate without the need for words.

'I hear you met Tom,' she said at last.

'Yes.' And suddenly he was the one who was finding it difficult to speak.

'He's staying over at Sarah's tonight, just in case... Well, just in case. There's always a chance of a heart attack.'

He knew that too. It was what his grandmother had finally succumbed to, but he didn't tell her that. Instead he said, 'Don't be alone, Fleur. Any problem, I can be with you in minutes.'

'Matt...' He waited, smiling as he heard her muttering to herself, as if trying out the words before she said them out loud, blissfully unaware that he could hear her every word. 'The reason I called is because, well, I wanted you to know that I've told Dad everything. I wanted him to know about us. How long we'd known one another. About how we got married.' She paused. 'That Tom is your son.'

Just in case she didn't get another chance, he knew. He didn't say that either. Some things didn't need words.

'How did he take it?'

'A few unsteady bleeps on the life support system, but on the whole very calmly. Of course he was sedated,' she added, and he could hear the smile in her voice.

'I'm sure that helped.'

'No. He was okay. Really.' She managed a smile. 'No, you're right, it must have been the sedatives.'

'Did he say anything?'

'He just wanted to know if I'd loved you.'

And suddenly his own heart was beating unsteadily. 'What did you tell him?'

He'd heard her, but he wanted her to tell him.

'The truth, Matt. Nothing but the truth.'

His turn to swallow.

'I told him the whole story. Right from when I poked my tongue at you through a gap in the fence when I was about five. He seemed to understand.' Then, with that slightly forced brightness, 'Anyway, I wanted to tell you that you can tell your mother about us, about Tom, whenever you want.'

'I'll give you due warning.'

'I'd appreciate that.'

'And Tom? When do we tell him?'

'He told me all about meeting you this afternoon. He was deeply impressed by your hedge-trimmer.' The smile was back. 'In fact he said that we should invite you to tea to say thank you for all your hard work.'

'He said that?'

'To tell you the truth, I think Sarah might have put him up to it. I suspect she fancies herself as matchmaker.'

'I think she's rather further along than that.'

'What? You mean she knows? She told you?'

'She didn't say a word, but I'd stake Hanovers against Gilberts that she sent the cutting.'

'She never said a word to me. In fact, only this morning she was...'

'What?'

'Nothing.'

'Are you angry with her?'

'No…' Then, 'No, Matt. Of course I'm not angry.'

'Good. Tell Tom that I'd love to come to tea any time.'

'Right, well, I'll…um…let you know. When.'

Fleur disconnected, put the phone down, rubbed her hands over her face in an attempt to erase the picture in her head of Matt lying back in his bath, his broad shoulders completely filling one end of the tub, a frill of foam clinging to satiny skin. Doing her best to ignore a deep yearning to be up to her neck in hot water with him.

Instead she dragged herself upstairs and, after the minimum basics in the bathroom, set the alarm for six the next morning and then fell into bed.

No sooner had her head hit the pillow than the irritating little peep-peep-peep, peep-peep-peep, peep-peep-peep dragged her back to consciousness. It was barely light. She could hear the rain pelting against the window. She groped for the clock, couldn't find the button to shut it up, and stuffed it under the heap of pillows to muffle it. Ten more minutes. She just had to have ten more minutes…

When she opened her eyes again the rain had stopped and watery sunlight was filtering into the room. She stretched, turned to check the clock. And remembered.

It was nearly eight o'clock.

She'd lost two hours, two hours she'd desperately needed. Each one of the show plants had to be turned a quarter each day to ensure they grew evenly. There were hundreds of them and it took for ever.

She had to phone the hospital.

She had to check all the glasshouses, the pumps, the misters, the heating system. All of which had been neglected yesterday.

She flew down the stairs, pulling her sweats over her pyjamas, not bothering with her hair, not bothering to stop and grab breakfast or even a cup of tea as she rushed through the kitchen, punching in the fast dial for the hospital as she ran.

'Hello?' She paused to catch her breath, opening the glasshouse door. 'Ward Six? This is Fleur Gilbert, I'm calling about my father—'

She came to an abrupt halt.

'Matt?'

Matt looked up briefly from the staging but he didn't stop work, moving slowly along as he turned each plant, checking it briefly for any of a dozen things that might presage trouble.

'What are you doing?' she asked, as if it wasn't plainly obvious. He was doing what she'd been planning to get up early to do herself. And the fact that he was well advanced with the job suggested that when his alarm had gone off he hadn't turned over and gone back to sleep.

'With your dad in hospital, I thought you might welcome a hand with this.'

'Miss Gilbert? Are you there, Miss Gilbert?'

She stopped trying to figure out what was happening and gave her attention to the nurse on the other end of the telephone who assured her that her father had had a comfortable night.

'Okay?' Matt asked.

'Comfortable. They're doing tests and stuff this morning. They said to leave visiting until this afternoon.'

'Right. Do you want a cup of coffee?'

'What?'

Matt indicated a large Thermos on her father's work table behind her.

'I don't suppose you're looking for a job, are you?' she asked as she unscrewed the plastic cups and poured coffee into one of them.

'That depends. What incentives are you offering?'

On the point of telling him that he could have whatever he wanted, including her, naked, on the staging, the scent of hot coffee began to penetrate her fuddled brain. It wasn't her he was interested in. It was Tom. So, rather than making a complete fool of herself, she raised the Thermos and said, 'Coffee?'

CHAPTER NINE

'COFFEE will do for now,' Matt said, turning back to the bench, continuing with what he was doing. 'No need for you to hang around; I'll check the systems for you when I've done this.' Then, as Fleur placed the coffee beside him, 'If you got a bustle on you could go and give Tom a good morning hug before he goes into school.'

Fleur tucked her hair behind her left ear, her feelings a confused muddle on a roller coaster ride. Her first thought on seeing him standing in her father's place had not been anger, but a wild, foolish surge of joy. First the hedges, now this. He'd seen what had to be done and had just got on with it. It was the way she'd always dreamed it would be, the two of them working together as a team.

And he seemed to have sorted out what Tom needed, too. To feel safe, secure.

And that was the downside. The minute he'd mentioned Tom she'd known that his apparent change of heart had nothing to do with her. This was about demonstrating just how useless she was. How feeble her father was. How much better off his son would be with him.

'Actually, I think I will, if you really don't mind me abandoning you?' she said, and then mentally flinched, certain he'd think she'd chosen the word deliberately.

But he shook his head, apparently not noticing her slip. But then why would he mind? What possible reason could he have for wanting to spend a moment longer than necessary with a woman who didn't bother to comb her hair, get properly dressed, before starting work?

Some businesswoman.

She scalded her mouth in an attempt to finish the coffee quickly so that she could escape. Then, having set the cup down, she backed towards the door, not wanting to take her eyes off him a moment before she had to. Watching him work down the line of pots, lift check, turn, replace… It must have been years since he'd done anything like that and yet he did it with the perfect economy of movement, the ease of someone completely at home with what he was doing.

She wanted to say something, to somehow let him know what she was feeling, but then he really would be in control. Not just of a row of pots, but of her, of Tom, of everything.

'I'll see you later, I expect,' she said finally, wanting him to look up. Look at her. See her. Remember, the way she was remembering.

Matt's hands were shaking. From the moment Fleur had burst into the glasshouse, her hair wild, her pyjama top sticking out from beneath an old grey sweatshirt, not a scrap of make-up or artifice, he'd been on a knife-edge. He wanted her so much. Wanted to just reach for her, no questions, no hesitation, the way it had always been from the first moment he'd taken her into his arms, their perfect connection transcending the need for anything as cumbersome as words.

He'd buried his feelings so deep, had concentrated his whole being on building an empire of his own that no one could ever take from him, that he'd actually believed he didn't care about her. That he had nothing to return for.

Then that newspaper cutting had arrived and overturned his world.

And now he knew that it had only been pride, stubborn, stupid pride, that had kept him away for so long.

He gripped the pot he was holding. It didn't matter what she'd done, or who she'd done it with, he still wanted her more than any woman on earth and, whatever it took, he was going to make it his business to show her that.

'Fleur...' He turned, looked up.

She was looking at him instead of what she was doing, unaware of what was happening behind her. Before he could warn her, she overreached, the door opened behind her and she fell back, straight into the arms of Charlie Fletcher.

'Charlie!'

She flushed, looking as guilty as a child caught with her hand in the cookie jar. 'I didn't know you were back.'

Charlie Fletcher held her, his hands gripping the tops of her arms long after the need to stop her from falling had passed.

'I just heard about your dad. Why didn't you call me? I'd have come straight back if I'd known you needed me. What can I do...?' He stopped as he realised that they weren't alone and Matt saw the shock register as Fletcher recognised him. Saw him look down at Fleur, absorb her dishevelled appearance, leap to conclusions. Saw his hands bite possessively into Fleur's arms before he continued. 'Tell me what I can do for you, Fleur.'

Matt wanted to hit him, tear the man's hands off her, but inside his head a voice was saying, *Six years. You walked out on her and didn't write or phone for nearly six years...*

Then the pot he was holding exploded in his hand, show-ering compost, fragments of plastic and potential Gold Medal winning fuchsia over the diamond pattern of black and terra-cotta tiles that had been laid when Queen Victoria was on the throne.

Fleur had been standing with her back to Matt, but she'd been able to feel his eyes burning into her, taking full note of the way Charlie was holding her. As if he had the right, as if he owned her. Despite her assurance that they were 'just good friends' she knew exactly how this must look to Matt. He wouldn't need the sly innuendo of the village gossip mill to point him in the right direction.

And for the first time she wondered if Charlie himself, call-ing round to spend time with her father, do little jobs for her, had been reading more into their friendship than she had ever intended.

Seizing the distraction offered by the shattered flowerpot, Fleur disengaged herself from Charlie's grip, grabbed a new pot and a handful of compost and set about saving the plant, while Matt and Charlie glared at one another along the length of the glasshouse.

'Matt?' she asked, in an effort to lighten the atmosphere. 'Are you okay? Did you cut yourself?'

He shook his head. 'I'm fine. I wish I could say the same about the plant.'

'It's ruined,' Charlie said accusingly.

'It takes more than that to destroy a fuchsia,' Fleur assured him shakily, making a vague gesture between the two of them, jabbing furiously at a wayward strand of hair that re-fused to stay out of the way behind her ear. 'You remember Matt Hanover, don't you, Charlie?'

He nodded once. 'I'd heard you were back.'

'Some news travels faster than others, it seems,' Matt said. Then, 'Could you come in or go out, Fletcher, and whichever you decide, close the door. You're causing a draught.'

Fleur glared at him, then glared at Charlie for good measure before setting the new pot back on the staging. 'If you'll both excuse me, I really do have to get dressed,' she said, then belatedly realised that Charlie would probably read a lot more into that simple statement than she meant, too.

She didn't hang around to find out but slipped through the open doorway and ran back towards the house.

'Fleur, wait!'

'Charlie, I have a lot to do.'

'Did he stay here last night? With your father in hospital?'

Her first reaction was to deny it. Do what she'd been doing all her life. Deny it. Hide her feelings. Kowtow to a feud that had nothing to do with her, or Matt. If she'd had the courage to match her love, to stand up to her parents, defy his, her dream would have stood a chance.

She'd made her choices and so had he, and they had to live with them. But it was not too late for Tom. He was entitled to know who he was. Know his history.

It was time to step out of the shadows. Now. This minute. Her father knew the truth and soon everyone else would and, standing up as straight as she knew how, she said, 'I'm sorry, Charlie, but I don't actually think that's any of your business.'

'Of course it's my business,' he said, as if puzzled by her reaction. 'I understood that you needed time, but I've been patient. Taken care of you. I'd have given you anything, you must know that. All you had to do was lift your little finger and I'd have been there.'

'Charlie...' She shivered as a chill wind cut through her

thin sweats. 'I'm sorry. I had no idea you felt that way. I value you friendship, truly, but Matt and I—'

'Matt and you?' His expression darkened. 'There can be no "Matt and you". He's a Hanover—'

'So is Fleur, Fletcher,' Matt said, coming up behind him. 'So is Fleur.'

Charlie continued to stare at her, uncomprehending.

'We were married nearly six years ago,' he continued, hammering home the point, ignoring her whispered 'No', her instinctive gesture as she attempted to claw the words back, make them unsaid, realising belatedly that Charlie wouldn't be able to cope. 'Fleur is my wife. Tom is my son.' Then, as Charlie continued to stare at her, 'Are you all right, Fleur?'

'All right?' Charlie turned on him. 'How can she possibly be all right?'

Fleur cried out as he swung his fist, but Matt made no move to defend himself or avoid the blow, taking it, staggering back under the weight of it, only lifting his hand to his mouth when the other man had turned and walked stiffly away.

'Matt! Oh, good grief!' Fleur pulled up her sweatshirt and used the tail of her pyjama jacket to staunch the blood. She was shaking like an aspen. 'You deserved that!' she said furiously, dabbing at his split lip. 'The pair of you behaved like a couple of Neanderthals. Whatever possessed you? You could see how upset he was!'

'He was the one who behaved like a Neanderthal, but I could see he needed to hit something and thought it was probably best if it was me.'

She stopped dabbing at his lip. Frowned.

'Charlie wouldn't hurt me.'

'I saw the way he held you, Fleur.' He reached out, lightly touched her arm. 'You'll have bruises.'

'He just grabbed me to stop me from falling,' she declared. She didn't want to hear what Matt was saying.

'And I saw his face when he followed you. The quiet, obsessive ones are always the most dangerous.'

'Obsessive? No.' She paused. 'He's never made any kind of a move, not so much as a kiss on the cheek.'

'He didn't have any competition. He thought you were all his.'

'No! He had no right. I didn't give him any encouragement…'

'He told the person I sent to make enquiries about Gilberts, about Tom, about you, that you were going to marry him—'

'In his dreams!' Then she realised that that was exactly the situation. 'Oh, good grief. That's awful. I feel so bad.'

'You don't have to feel anything, Fleur.'

She swallowed, then, because she didn't want to think about all the times he'd turned up to work on one of his caravans when she'd been alone with Tom, she said, 'I suppose I should at least be grateful that you didn't hit him back.'

'It's a one-time deal. Next time he lays a hand on you, he gets what's coming to him.'

'He won't get the chance.' Firmly changing the subject, she said, 'So. You sent someone to snoop around the village. Ask about me.'

'I needed to know what I was coming back to. Six years is a long time, and you had every right—'

'All you had to do was pick up a telephone and ask, Matt.' She stepped back, putting some distance between them.

She wasn't sure whether she wanted to laugh or cry. In

the end she did neither, just said, 'We need to get some ice on your lip.'

As she applied half a pack of frozen beans to Matt's mouth, she asked herself out loud, 'How could I have missed the way Charlie felt about me? Not have seen the danger? I didn't mean to hurt him.'

'I know.'

'You do?'

'I had this girl working in my office when I first set up on my own in Hungary. Katya. She was a terrific organiser. Quick, bright, clever—'

'Beautiful?'

He smiled. 'That, too.' Then, 'Ouch!'

'Sorry.'

'If I'm going to tell you the rest of this, I think I should be in charge of the ice pack,' he said. Once she'd relinquished it, he went on, 'About a year after she joined my company, I took her to the Paris agricultural show with me. When we arrived at the hotel I discovered she'd only booked one room.'

'Oh, dear,' she said, mock tragic, wishing she hadn't been so quick to give up her only weapon. 'That must have been a real problem. Whatever did you do?'

'I tried to be kind, but she was embarrassed, angry, clearly felt utterly stupid. All the things Charlie Fletcher is feeling right now.'

'Including the sore knuckles?'

He shrugged. 'All creatures lash out when they're hurt. You're cold, Fleur. Go and have a hot shower.'

'Matt…' He waited. 'You told Charlie about us. That we're married.'

'I don't suppose he'll be rushing to the village shop to

spread the news. He'll need time to lick his wounds, get used to the idea. With luck he'll convince himself he knew the truth all along.'

'Possibly, but it'll be a miracle if the entire village hasn't heard a whisper before the end of the week.'

'Do you mind?'

She shook her head. 'I wasn't thinking about myself. I was thinking about your mother. You might want to tell her the truth before she hears it from someone else.'

'I'll see to it as soon as I've finished the plants. Thanks for the first aid,' he said, standing up and handing her the bag of soggy beans.

'You're welcome.'

Matt didn't want to put an end to their unexpected closeness but there was nothing else to say. He returned to the glasshouse to continue the tedious job that would have to be done every day until the Chelsea Flower Show.

With her father out of commission she'd need someone to take care of that and it was something practical he could do to help, he decided, glancing along the staging, estimating how much longer it would take, before letting his mind drift back to the incident with Katya.

She'd called him every name she could lay her tongue to, he remembered. Had impugned his manhood. Had implied that he was impotent. Worse, she'd made him feel embarrassed, even foolish, for being so meticulously faithful to an absent wife, and he'd blamed Fleur for somehow emasculating him.

A real man didn't turn down a beautiful woman when she offered herself up on a plate, did he?

Actually, yes.

Because Fleur had not emasculated him. On the contrary,

she'd given him the part of himself that had been missing until he'd met her.

And he smiled as he replaced the last plant, because the beauty of it was that it had worked both ways. The reason she'd been blind to Charlie Fletcher's obsession was because he'd done the same for her.

Only together could they ever be truly whole.

'Is my mother around, Lucy?'

'No, Matt. She called from the house first thing and asked me to cancel her appointments. She said she had something she had to do today.'

'No clues as to what that might be? When she'll be back?'

'Nothing.' She looked as if she might say more and he waited. 'To tell you the truth, Matt, she did seem very upset yesterday afternoon. I suspect it had something to do with you cutting the Gilberts' hedge.'

'Oh?'

'I thought she was on the phone, but when I came into the office she was actually talking to herself. She'd been watching you from the window and when she turned around, I could see she was crying.'

'Crying?'

He'd never seen his mother shed a tear in his entire life. Not for a pet dog, not when she'd broken her wrist, not when his father had died.

'I asked her if there was something wrong, but she said no.'

'You weren't convinced.' She shook her head. 'I don't suppose you overheard what she was saying to herself, Lucy?' She shrugged, clearly reluctant to say any more. 'It could be important.'

'I didn't catch much, just something about Seth having to

pay for it. I half expected her to tell me to raise an invoice, charge Mr Gilbert for the hedge work.'

Fleur, working her way through the mail and hyperventilating over an offer for the barn from a client of Martin and Lord, would normally have left the answering machine to pick up the call but, knowing that it might be the hospital, she snatched it up. 'Fleur Gilbert.'

'Fleur?'

Something about the urgency with which he said her name caught her attention. 'Matt? Is something wrong?'

'You haven't had any trouble?'

'Trouble? Are you still worried about Charlie? He hasn't been near.'

'No—'

'In fact, it's been a very good morning so far. The surveyor—'

'Fleur!' Then, when she paused, 'Not with Fletcher, with my mother. Has she been there?'

'Oh! Well, no.' Then, 'I take it she didn't respond at all well to the prospect of being related by blood to a Gilbert?'

'I haven't seen her or spoken to her, but I was hard on her yesterday and I'm a bit concerned. Stay in the house, I'm on my way over.'

'But—'

But he'd already hung up and he must have already been on his way when he'd called because it was less than five minutes before he tapped on the back door and called out, 'It's Matt.'

'Come on in, it's open.'

'When I said stay inside…' he said, when he finally found her still sitting exactly where she'd been when he'd called, still transfixed by the letter from Martin and Lord, staring at it as if she couldn't believe her eyes. Well, she couldn't. '…I meant stay inside with the door locked.'

She frowned. 'Don't be silly. Your mother is a pain in the derrière, but she isn't violent.' Then, because he didn't immediately agree, she looked up. 'What's happened?'

'I don't know. But she's not in the office and yesterday afternoon Lucy overheard her muttering about your father having to pay.'

'What for?'

'I don't know, Fleur, but she was crying—'

She didn't wait for more, but dropped the letter, picked up her bag, then picked up the letter and put it inside the bag and still beat him to the door. 'Come on.'

'Where are you going?'

'To the hospital.'

'But why?' Matt said, heading for his car, opening the door for her. It said a lot for her state of mind that she slid, without argument, into the soft leather luxury rather than insisting on taking her own aged transport, but she didn't have time for such nonsense.

'Because that's where my father is,' she said impatiently. 'Isn't this thing supposed to go faster than this?'

'Not when there's a forty mile an hour speed limit. Anyway, it's not visiting time. They won't let her in.'

'You want to bet?'

And while he drove as fast as the law allowed to the hospital, she attempted to contact the ward sister, find out if Katherine Hanover was there.

'It's engaged,' she said. Then, 'Tell me exactly what your mother said.'

'I don't know *exactly*. Only what Lucy thought she overheard.'

'And she was crying? Is that significant?'

He glanced at her. 'I've never seen my mother cry. Not even when Dad died.'

She reached out, put her hand over his. 'I'm sure it's nothing. Really.'

'Are you? You were the one who pointed out that her animosity towards the Gilberts was odd.'

'I know, but honestly, Matt. Think about it. What is she going to do to him?'

And then she was the one thinking about him lying there, partially paralysed, unable to speak clearly, and she tried the hospital again.

Matt dropped Fleur at the entrance. By the time he'd found somewhere to park and caught up with her she was arguing with a nurse that she had to see her father. Now.

'Come back at two, Miss Gilbert. You can stay for as long as you like then.'

'Please, I have to see him *now!*'

'One minute, nurse?' he asked. 'My wife just needs one minute to reassure herself.'

'I'm reassuring her. Her father had a comfortable night, but he's had a whole battery of tests this morning and he's asleep.'

Behind her a monitor began to bleep loudly. While she was distracted, summoning the crash trolley, a doctor, Fleur took off and he was close on her heels when she came to an abrupt halt at the door to her father's room.

His mother was sitting beside Seth Gilbert. Not saying anything. Just sitting there, watching him.

'Mum?'

She turned her head as if it weighed almost more than she

could bear, stared at him for a moment as if she didn't know who he was.

'Mum, what are you doing here?'

'Shh. He's asleep.'

'What have you done to him?' Fleur demanded, rushing to his side, wanting to see for herself that he was breathing. Then, once she was satisfied, 'How did you get in here?'

'I just walked in. Everyone was busy.' She turned to look down at him. 'Seth and I have been talking. It's been so long since I talked to him.'

'Mum—'

'You should have told me he was in hospital, Matt.'

'Why?' Fleur interjected. 'So that you could gloat? The way you came to gloat over my mother?'

Fleur felt Matt's hand seize hers as he tried to pull her away.

'Sweetheart, please…'

'She just walked in, Matt. Apparently she'd just been to identify your father's body, so the charitable view was that she wasn't thinking straight, but when my father heard her he collapsed. Even then, when he finally managed to speak, he said not to blame her.' She turned on Katherine. 'No matter what you did, he never would have said a word against you.'

'Fleur…'

'My mother was terribly burned, Matt, before they got her out of the car—'

'Please, don't do this to yourself.'

'Let her speak, Matt.'

'She came up to the intensive care unit and stood there for a while, with me and my father, looking at my mother through the glass wall. I assumed that she'd come to offer some comfort to him, as a fellow victim, but all she said was, "I hope she lives. I want her to live, to feel some of the pain she's put me through all these years."'

Katherine Hanover covered her mouth with her hand, moaning softly.

'Tell him it's true,' Fleur said.

'Yes. Yes, God forgive me…'

'Fleur,' Matt said, 'please, come away now.'

'And leave my father with her?' She turned on him. 'If you'd been there, Matt. If you'd heard her. How could I go with you after that?'

'I know, love,' he said, 'I know.' And opened his arms to her.

CHAPTER TEN

MATT pulled Fleur against him, holding her, absorbing the shuddering sobs into his body, feeling each one like a blow.

Over her head his gaze connected with his mother's. She looked grey, years older than the perfectly groomed woman who had seemed such a stranger to him.

He recognised this unhappy woman, finally understood that she had been unhappy all her married life, and it was clear to him from the way she looked at Seth that, whatever she'd done, she was the one who'd paid.

'Out!' The nurse, emergency over, had finally caught up with them. 'All of you!'

Seth Gilbert tried to speak.

'It's all right, Seth,' the nurse said, straightening a cover. 'Take your time.'

Fleur, ignoring the nurse, pulled away from Matt's arms, reaching out to take her father's hand, and Matt had to fight a rush of despair. He'd lost her to her father once before, because his need had been the greater.

'What is it, Dad?' she asked gently. 'What do you want?'

Again Seth struggled to speak.

'I can't…' Fleur turned to look at him then, and Matt felt

the despair evaporate. It was different this time. This time he was there for her. At her side. 'I don't understand,' she said helplessly.

'He wants me to stay.' They both turned to look at Matt's mother. 'He's saying that he wants me to stay,' she repeated, her face lit with wonder as he took his hand from Fleur's and reached out for her.

'I know,' Fleur said, looking to him for an answer. 'I know what he said, Matt. That's what I don't understand.'

'Neither do I,' he replied, 'but they do and that's all that matters.'

'Five minutes,' the nurse conceded, since it was clear that nothing was going to move Katherine Hanover short of calling Security, something that would obviously cause more disruption than one out-of-hours visitor. And, pointing at Katherine, she said, 'Just you. Five minutes. No more.'

'We'll be in the cafeteria, Mum.' For a moment Fleur dug in her heels, stubbornly refusing to move. 'They need to talk, Fleur, and so do we.'

With his arm at her back, she finally allowed herself to be directed towards the hospital cafeteria, where Matt eased her into a chair as if she were the invalid, before going to fetch a couple of cups of something brown and warm. She didn't ask what it was. She didn't actually care.

'He held her hand, Matt.'

'I saw. He's on the mend, Fleur. Soon he'll be up and dancing.'

'With your mother?' She shook her head. 'He wanted her there.' She looked up then. 'I didn't even know he knew her.'

'She told me the other day that she used to go to parties thrown by your grandmother.'

'You didn't tell me.'

'No, well, she was offering me your house at the time. As an incentive to settle down.'

'Oh, she was, was she?' Fleur finally managed a smile. 'I'm sorry to disappoint both of you, but reports of our imminent bankruptcy are greatly exaggerated.' And to prove it she opened her bag and showed him the letter she'd received from Martin and Lord, with its eye-watering offer for the barn. 'Your surveyor wasn't kidding when he said he knew someone who'd buy the place.' She waited while he read it. 'You'll note that the offer isn't subject to planning permission.'

He handed the letter back to her. 'Will you take it?'

'Well, yes. We'll have to.'

'Good.' There was nothing wrong with his reaction and yet she felt oddly flattened by it. She didn't know what she'd expected. A little more emotion, perhaps. A little sadness that a place that had been so special to them would be transformed beyond recognition.

Stupid.

She sipped the drink he'd brought her, more for something to do than because she really wanted it.

'More sweet tea,' she said. 'I'll have to take care or I might get to like it.' Then, because she couldn't help herself, 'You called me your wife. When you spoke to the nurse.'

'It seemed simpler,' he said, 'although it's scarcely true any more, is it?'

'No, I suppose not.'

For a moment they sat opposite one another, both lost in their thoughts, then, as a shadow fell over the table, he looked up, stood up. 'Mother.'

Katherine Hanover remained standing, almost Fleur thought as if she was waiting for permission to join them.

'Please sit down, Mrs Hanover.'

'Thank you.'

'Would you like something to drink? Matt does a good line in hot sweet tea.'

Matt didn't wait for her response, but crossed to the counter, leaving them alone.

'Seth tells me that you and Matt…that Tom is my grandson.'

Fleur swallowed. 'Yes.'

'I've seen him, you know. Watched him playing in your garden just the way Matt did when he was a little boy. It was like looking back at something precious. Raising Matt was the one good thing I did.' She smiled. 'Tom is a fine boy. A credit to you.'

'Thank you.' Then, 'What happened, Mrs Hanover? Between you and my father. Can you tell me?'

'You've a right to know.'

Matt put a cup in front of his mother, sat down beside Fleur, took her hand. Katherine didn't appear to notice. She seemed to be in another place, another time. Remembering.

At last she said, 'Jennifer, your mother, was my best friend.'

'Oh.'

'We went everywhere together, a whole group of us. Phillip, Seth, all of us.'

Fleur frowned. 'But what about the feud?'

'It was little more than a joke. Something to give an extra edge to competition, whether it was business or just a village darts match for the older generation. For us, well, it was ancient history.'

She sat for a while, her mind clearly back in the past, remembering how it had been. 'Phillip was absolutely besotted with Jennifer, and she was leading him on although I knew she wasn't really interested. When I challenged her about it she said she waiting for Mr Right to notice her, but in the meantime he was good-looking, had the kind of sports car that girls like to be seen in.'

Fleur recognised this painful portrait of her mother. About as deep as an August puddle.

'I was in love with Seth. I wanted him so much that I ached with it, but things were different then. Sex was something that only bad girls did and Jennifer encouraged me to keep my distance, play it cool. And she certainly had Phillip on leading strings, so I thought she must know what she was talking about.'

'It didn't work.'

'That depends on your point of view. Seth got a bit carried away one night at a party. I wanted him, heaven knows I wanted him, but boys like Seth didn't marry girls who were easy and I was playing for keeps. He took it badly. Things were said in the heat of the moment, shocking things, and I ended up sobbing in Jennifer's arms. She said she'd talk to him, sort things out. Tell him how much I loved him. How stupid he'd been.'

Fleur tried to imagine her father as a young man in the throes of passion but, fortunately, couldn't manage it.

'I take it she didn't manage to convince him.'

'She didn't even try. What she actually told him was that I was a baby. That I needed to grow up. Stroked his bruised ego, told him that a good-looking man like him could have anybody. Could have her.'

'Why?'

'Because she could. She was a beautiful girl, Fleur.'

'Not inside.'

'No. To be honest, thinking about it with the twenty-twenty vision of hindsight, I think she was just plain annoyed that

Seth Gilbert wanted her boring, rather plain little friend when she was ready, willing and available. I didn't see it that way at the time, of course. She cried when she told me what had happened.'

'She cried very easily.'

'They took a bottle of wine down to the old barn, talked for hours about me, she said.' Katherine managed a bleak smile. 'The fact that she told me they'd gone to the barn was enough. It was where everyone went to make out back then.'

Matt's fingers tightened on Fleur's as if warning her not to say anything.

Maybe Katherine saw, because she smiled. 'Obviously I'm not telling you two anything.' Then, 'Jennifer swore she never meant it to happen, but too much drink, too much emotion, had inevitably spilled over into something else. That she was pregnant with Seth's baby—'

'What? No!'

'No. It was a lie, of course. But I was distraught and Phillip was hurting too. We clung to each other for comfort, but by the time I discovered the truth, that Jennifer wasn't pregnant, that Seth hadn't gone anywhere with her, it was too late. I was carrying you, Matt, and back then there was only one answer. Marriage.'

'Oh, dear God.' As the words escaped Matt's lips his fingers dug into her hand and she welcomed the pain.

'We made the best of it because we had to. It might have worked if we'd been somewhere else. If Jennifer hadn't been married to Seth. If she hadn't discovered, too late, that Phillip really had been the man she loved all along.'

'Mum—'

Fleur knew Matt was thinking of her, that she wouldn't want to hear this about her own mother, but Katherine had had it bottled up for so long that nothing would stop her. And actually Fleur didn't want to stop her. Katherine Hanover needed her outpouring of grief, because that was what it was, grief for a lost life. And she really needed to hear it. All of it. The whole truth.

'I hated her so much. And him. He knew what she'd done and I couldn't understand how he could have married her after that. But I see now that I was as much to blame. I believed her, even when she'd told me he'd acted in a way that seemed so utterly against his nature. Trust. In the end all you have is trust. He'd denied he'd been with Jennifer, but I just didn't trust him.'

'Why did he marry her?' Fleur asked.

'He told me this morning that he'd lost the only woman he'd ever loved, so it didn't actually matter who he married. And Jennifer swore that she'd only lied to break us up because she loved him so much. It was, he thought, the best he could hope for.'

And with that so many things slipped into place. Her parents' apparent lack of any genuine affection for one another. The fact that her father had never seemed to care whether his wife was there or not, leaving her to buy the happiness he was unable to give her.

Katherine Hanover looked up then. 'We've messed up your lives too, haven't we?'

Fleur didn't know what to say, but Matt reached out, took his mother's hand. 'No, Mum, I managed that without any help from you, but we're working on it.'

They were? She looked at him and said, 'No, Matt. It wasn't just you.'

Katherine nodded, apparently content. 'That's a start.' Then, 'Seth is going to need a lot of care when he comes home and you've got the business to run, Chelsea to organise.'

'I'm taking care of Chelsea,' Matt said.

'*You are?*' Fleur found it was easier to get the question out when it involved ordinary old business rather than her heart and soul.

'If you'll let me.'

'Well, good. Good,' Katherine said, as if that was settled. Then, after a pause, 'I have no right to ask this, Fleur, but will you let me take care of Seth? When he comes out of hospital. Give me a chance to put things right?'

'We all deserve that, Mrs Hanover.'

'Katherine.' The confident, assured businesswoman, politician, had disappeared and in her place was a woman pleading for understanding, her smile tentative. 'Please.'

And in that moment Fleur melted. 'Katherine,' she said.

'It all begins to make sense,' Fleur said. They'd left Katherine at the hospital; she'd wanted to stay. Be there. 'My parents never did have a close marriage. I'd never really thought about it before, but looking back, I actually don't think they could stand one another at the end. He spent all his time trying to breed his precious yellow fuchsia. She went through money like water. It was as if she was trying to ruin my father. And he did nothing to stop her.'

'You have to pity them all.'

'Even my mother?'

'Even her.'

'You're too generous, Matt. I can quite easily see why your mother would hate her.'

'I think she's just learned that it's a waste of time living in the past, feeding on old wounds.'

'Don't be too hard on her, Matt. It's time to put the past where it belongs, think of the future.'

'You're right.' He glanced at her. 'So when am I going to get this invitation to tea, Mrs Hanover?'

There was no drama, no need for difficult explanations, when Fleur, walking Tom home from school that evening, said, 'Tom, your daddy is coming to tea today.'

'Is he? Can we have fish fingers and ice cream?'

And then, when Matt arrived, Tom just grinned and said, 'Can I have a go with your hedge-trimmer?'

'I didn't bring it with me, Tom. I've got a football, though. Want to show me what you can do?'

They went outside and kicked a ball around on the grass driving Cora demented with excitement, while Fleur cried all over the fish fingers.

Later, when Matt had read Tom a bedtime story and tucked him up, the boy frowned and said, 'Will you come and see us again, Daddy, or do you have to go on another adventure?' And it was Matt's turn to struggle with tears.

'I'm going to be here all the time from now on, Tom.'

'Okay.'

'Adventure?' he asked, when they were safely downstairs, standing awkwardly in the front hall.

'When he asked where his daddy was, I said you were away having adventures.' She pulled her lips back against her teeth for a moment. 'I was reading him the *Adventures of Sinbad* at the time, so be prepared to be inventive about the monsters and demons you've fought.'

'Thanks for that.'

'You're a hero. Don't let him down.' Then, 'Matt...'

He waited.

'What you said to Tom about being here all the time...'

'Yes?'

Damn it, he must know what she was trying to say, it would be great if he helped her out. Or maybe that was the point. After the way he'd suggested she keep him occupied with sex while he was waiting for his son, maybe she had to be the one to say it.

'You don't have to go.'

He reached up, briefly touched her cheek, said, 'Yes, Fleur. I do.' Then, as if to prove it, he opened the front door, stepped through before turning to face her. 'Have you spoken to Derek Martin yet about the offer for the barn?'

Her face flamed in embarrassment. She'd just propositioned her husband and been turned down.

She swallowed, struggled to unstick her tongue from the roof of her mouth, finally managed a croaky, 'Things have changed, Matt. Dad may not want to sell now.'

'He doesn't have much choice.'

'He doesn't?'

'Your father might have found a lost love, Fleur, but he's still on the point of bankruptcy. Don't let sentiment get in the way of a good deal.'

'Heaven forbid that any of us should let sentiment dictate our actions,' she said, her voice oddly steady, even while her heart was sinking like a stone.

So much that had happened that day had been positive. Had she read into his words, his actions, more than he'd intended?

Heard only what she wanted to hear?

Of course she had. He'd come for Tom. She'd negotiated a few weeks to prepare her son, her father, but most of all herself, for the inevitable. In the event, he'd got everything he wanted in days rather than weeks. He didn't need her any more. 'Working on it' referred to the legal details, tying up the loose ends, that was all.

'There's no room for sentiment in business, Fleur. You

can't carry on the way you have been. It was hard enough before, but your father isn't going to be able to do much for some time. You need to think about the future, talk to him about where Gilberts is going.'

Easy for him to say, but when you were working as hard as you could simply to keep your head above water, it was difficult to look ahead, make plans.

When she didn't answer, he said, 'I've got one or two ideas. If you want to talk, just give me a call.' He went on, before she could say anything, 'I'll be here first thing tomorrow to look after the Show plants.'

She wanted to say, Don't bother, I can manage, but the truth was, she couldn't. And he knew it.

'Have you got transport organised? Help in the marquee?' he asked.

'Charlie was going to…' she began in her desperation to prove that she wasn't a complete no-hoper. But clearly that was no longer an option. 'I guess not.'

'Don't worry about it. I can organise all that.'

She only just stopped herself from blurting out, Why? Why are you doing this?

She knew why. It wasn't for her, but for his son. The new cultivar was a historic breakthrough. Gilbert's Gold was Tom's birthright.

'Thank you, Matt,' she managed. Then shivered. 'I appreciate that.'

'You're cold.' He looked up at the clear sky. 'There's going to be a frost tonight.' Then, when she didn't move, 'Go inside, Fleur.'

Too weary to argue, she closed the door before she completely forgot herself and begged him to stay.

She'd been so busy protecting her father, protecting Tom, that she hadn't thought to protect herself. Too late now, but she didn't have the right to feel sorry for herself, to waste time thinking about what might have been. Instead she took Matt's advice and immediately went to the phone to put a call through to Derek Martin to tell him that she'd accept the offer for the barn. At least money would no longer be a worry.

Before she could pick up the receiver, it rang.

'Fleur Gil—'

'You haven't forgotten that we've got a date tomorrow, have you, Fleur?'

Matt. He couldn't have reached the gate before he'd called her on his mobile.

'A date?'

'Our first date, if I'm not very much mistaken.'

'You don't count all those nights in the barn, then?'

'Those weren't dates, Fleur. You probably don't know this, but the way it's supposed to work is that boy calls girl and asks her out. Boy picks up girl at front door. Boy delivers girl back to front door within the defined curfew, gets a goodnight kiss and goes home thinking he's one damn lucky man and planning his moves to get beyond a doorstep kiss.'

'You could have had anything you wanted tonight,' she reminded him. She knew it and he knew it too.

'Help me out here, Fleur. I'm only human. It took every bit of willpower to step back tonight.'

'Why did you?'

'Because I owe you that much.'

'Excuse me? I seem to have missed something.'

'You've missed out on a lot, Fleur. I want to make it up to you. To both of us. Let's do it the old-fashioned way this time.'

She clapped her hand over her mouth to stop the bubble of joy from escaping. To stop herself from telling him not to be so damn stupid and get right back there. She took a breath. This was more than a gesture; it was a new beginning, a new start.

'So,' she replied, blinking back tears, doing her best to sound cool. 'First we date? What did you have in mind?'

'I believe I mentioned that we had been invited to dinner at the Ravenscars' tomorrow evening.'

'I believe you did,' she replied.

'I may have been less than gracious when I asked you to join me.'

She struggled to contain a gurgle of laughter. 'I seem to recall that it was more in the nature of a command than an invitation.'

'I was rather hoping you'd forgotten exactly how less than gracious I'd been.'

'Did you? Why don't you ask me again, as if you really want me there?'

'I always wanted you there, Fleur, I just didn't know it.'

There were tears mingling with the laughter as she said, 'That's good enough. If I can organise a babysitter, I'd love to come.'

'No problem. I've already booked Lucy.'

'What? Isn't that taking my response for granted?'

'I wasn't about to take no for an answer. I'll pick you up at seven.'

The next day she found time to buy a dress she'd seen in a boutique in town. It was totally impractical but it went so perfectly with her amethyst earrings that she knew that it was the only one that would do for her 'first date' with Matt.

His face, when he came to pick her up, told her that she was right.

He didn't miss the earrings either and later, after he'd walked her to her door and she'd checked on Tom, and Lucy had left, he lifted one lobe so that the stone caught the light.

'I promised you that I'd replace these with diamonds one day.'

'Nothing could replace them,' she said.

'Maybe not, but I realised tonight that your left hand is looking a little bare. You took off your wedding ring as you left me that night. Did you ever wear it…after?'

'After you took off yours and tossed it into the hedge?'

'I never ceased to regret…'

She reached up, covered his mouth with her fingers. 'Sometimes,' she told him. 'On those nights when I went back to the barn, when I thought you might still come back. I have it safe.' Her voice was a little unsteady. 'I never quite gave up on you.' Then, taking her hand away, 'Do you want it back?'

'Your ring?'

'Yours. It took me weeks to find it…'

He didn't answer her, but instead took a box from his pocket, opened it to reveal a stunningly modern engagement ring with three oval diamonds set into a wide platinum band. 'Would this be a fair exchange? I saw it today and thought it would be perfect for you. If you don't agree, the jeweller will change it.'

He took it from the box and, taking her hand, slipped it on to her finger. She extended her hand, watching the light flash fire as she moved it slightly. Then, regretfully, she eased it off and returned it to him.

'You don't like it?'

'I love it, Matt. It's perfect.'

'Then…' He stopped. 'Oh, right. You want me on my knees, is that it?'

'This was your idea. You were the one who wanted to do it properly.'

'I wasn't sure you understood.'

'Oh, yes, Matt, I understand.' She understood that they'd both burn with need that night, but that some things were worth waiting for.

'So, tell me, Mrs Hanover,' he said, 'do I get a kiss on the first date?'

'Just one,' she said, lifting her arms and twining them about his neck. Then she smiled. 'So you'd better make it last.'

CHAPTER ELEVEN

FLEUR could not believe how quickly her father began to recover, how brilliantly he was responding to treatment; it was plain that it was entirely down to Katherine, who left her own business in Matt's more than capable hands so that she could spend hours talking to him, helping him with his exercises, his speech therapy.

She looked a different woman, Fleur thought, watching them together. She was still elegant, beautifully presented, but she'd lost that brittle edge. She looked both older and younger. Less Botox, more smiling, Fleur thought, when she sought her out, wanting to talk to her about the sale of the barn. She wanted to be completely open about it, not do anything to upset this special new accord.

'Katherine, I know you were interested in buying the barn, but I wanted you to know that I've got someone who will pay the market price.'

'Matt did mention something of the sort.'

She sent him a mental thank-you for making it so easy , but persisted, knowing the other woman was distracted, vulnerable. 'He said you were hoping to use it as a restaurant.' She knew that her father wouldn't want her to sell to someone else if Katherine really wanted it. 'Obviously the business needs the capital input, but I'm sure we could work something out.'

'You're very thoughtful, my dear. Far more than I deserve, but actually I've rethought my plans. The barn really is much too big for a restaurant.' She patted her arm distractedly. 'It'll make a much better home.'

'If you're sure. I have to admit it will get the bank manager off our backs.' For now, anyway.

Delia Johnson said much the same thing when she came out to the nursery to see for herself how things were going.

Packing was in full swing and, thanks to Matt, she had a glasshouse full of show quality plants nearing their peak. And when Ms Johnson still didn't look convinced, Fleur was able to produce a banker's draft for the full market price for the barn, which would wipe out their overdraft and leave a comfortable cushion of capital.

'Do you want to take it with you, Ms Johnson?' she asked. 'Or would you prefer me to transfer my overdraft to another bank?'

'I never wanted you to take your business elsewhere, Miss Gilbert. What I do want is some idea of how you plan to stop the slide. The next time you get into difficulties, you won't have the barn to bail you out, will you?'

'No,' she said. 'I suppose not.'

'You know, it would make sense to merge with Hanovers. They'd get the land they need for expansion and you'd have a cash-rich business to support your research.'

It made the most perfect sense. It was what she and Matt had planned all those years ago. But it was the one thing she couldn't suggest. He had to know that she wanted him for himself, not for his money.

* * *

'I could get used to dating,' Fleur said as Matt drove her and Tom home after the Easter weekend party at the Hallams' in the family car that had joined the sports car in his garage.

'Sweetheart, if you thought this afternoon was a date,' he said, glancing across at her, 'I've been getting something wrong.'

'You haven't been getting a single thing wrong,' she assured him, blushing.

After that first evening at the Ravenscars', which in retrospect had been wonderful, but at the time she'd been far too on edge to let herself go and enjoy, she'd loved every minute of it.

They'd done all the standard dates. The cinema, where they'd belatedly discovered the joys of squabbling amiably over whether they were going to watch a romantic comedy or a shoot-'em-up action movie at the cinema. As if it mattered. Sitting side by side, the only thing on either of their minds had been their closeness. Shoulders touching in the dark. Entwined fingers. The anticipation, the pleasure, the ultimate torture of saying goodnight. Of fulfilment postponed.

They'd taken Tom out on the river, eaten too much ice cream, held hands as they'd walked home without giving a hoot who saw them—and the sudden silence as she'd walked into the village shop the next day had assured her that they had been seen.

They'd gone to the village pub. Their appearance together had caused a brief hiatus in conversation, then someone had asked how her dad was, and then someone who'd been at school with Matt had challenged him to a game of darts, and by the end of the evening they had just been part of the crowd.

They'd spent time together, getting to know one another again, getting to know one another in ways they never had before. Cooking for each other. Working together. Spending time with Tom.

Then one night he took her to dinner in a restaurant perched high above the weir on the river at Maybridge. Despite the romantic setting he didn't talk of love, but of the life he'd built for himself in Hungary. His home there. The land. His business.

And suddenly she knew what he was going to say. That being married to him meant living where his life was.

'You make it sound so exciting,' she said. 'You must long to get back.'

'People are more important than places, Fleur. Where you are is my home.'

It was the moment of truth. To ask the question there was no avoiding. 'Me or Tom?'

He didn't rush to answer. Considered his words. 'I boarded that plane home so full of anger, rage, that it was a physical pain. When Amy Hallam came and sat beside me I almost exploded. I just wanted to be alone to let that anger grow, so that when I saw you I could be cruel, make you pay.'

She knew it, yet it still hurt to hear the words.

'I couldn't leave, Matt. Especially not with you. Not after what happened.'

'I should have understood that.'

'I should have tried to understand why you couldn't stay.'

'Communication. It's the glue that holds a relationship together. Our parents didn't have it and neither did we.'

'You talked to Amy.'

She tried not to feel envious of this woman who'd had the power to make him tell her how he felt.

'She talked to me, Fleur, and before I knew it I was showing her a photograph of you, the one of Tom in the school play. Talking about things I hadn't spoken of in years.'

'She's quite something, isn't she? It took me a while to work out who she is.'

Matt frowned. 'Who is she?'

'Amaryllis Jones. The woman who founded an empire on essential oils.'

'Oh. Right. That explains a lot. I was talking to one of my neighbours in Upper Haughton, Mike Armstrong—he was at the Ravenscars' with his wife?' She nodded. 'Well, he's known her for years and he's absolutely convinced that she's a witch.'

'Oh, what rot!' Then she paused, remembered the way Amy had spoken to her, touched her. Had made her feel as if she could do anything. They exchanged a look and burst out laughing.

Then Matt reached across the table to take both her hands in his and suddenly they weren't laughing any more. '"Come live with me, and be my love", Fleur,' he said, his eyes burning with a passion she'd never seen before, not even when he'd married her. Then, 'Oh, Lord, I had all this planned. I meant to have candles and roses and go down on my knees…'

'I never wanted you on your knees, Matt,' she said, turning her hands, grasping his. 'I'm your wife. We're partners. Always.' Then, fighting back tears, she told him, 'If you've got that ring handy, now would be a very good time.'

'Marry me, Fleur.'

'What? But we're—'

'In the village church, with the dress, the flowers, the top hats, bridesmaids, bells, choir, everyone we know. All the things we didn't have the first time.'

'Matt…I think you're forgetting something. We're already married.'

'Divorce me,' he declared fervently, drawing startled

glances from nearby diners, 'and we'll have a wedding that they'll still be talking about in Longbourne when our grand-children get married.'

Grandchildren? For a moment she covered her mouth with her hand, holding back the emotion. Then, at last, she said, 'We don't need a divorce, my love. Or even a wedding. We'll renew our vows, have a blessing. The only difference will be that we can walk up the aisle together.'

'That sounds about perfect to me,' he said. And this time when he took out the ring, slipped it on her finger, it stayed there.

'Fleur...'

She was buttering toast for Tom when Matt appeared at the kitchen door. She looked up, content as a cream-fed cat, sucked butter from her thumb, began to smile.

And then she saw his face. It was white.

'What is it?' she said. 'What's happened?' Then, 'Dad?'

'No!' He put his arms around her. 'No, it's not your father. It's the plants.'

She frowned. 'They were perfect last night. I checked them before I locked the glasshouses...'

She pulled free and, before he could stop her, ran to see for herself, coming to a halt as she reached the open door. Every plant had been destroyed. The pots had been overturned, the contents tipped out and trampled, ground into the tiled floor.

Matt put his arms around her, drew her against him. 'Who has a key?'

'A key?'

'The door was locked when I came to turn the plants. Whoever did this let themselves in with a key and locked up when he left.'

She shivered. 'You believe it was Charlie?'

'Did he have a key?'

'He sometimes helped Dad, but he wouldn't have given him a key to this glasshouse.'

'But he'd have had plenty of opportunity to have a copy made.'

'Why? Why would he do that?'

'Possessive, obsessive…' He drew in a sharp breath. 'This is my fault.'

'No!'

'My car was outside your front door all night. This is to punish you for what he sees as your betrayal.' She saw his fists clench. 'I'll put a stop to it right now—'

'No!' She held on to him. 'No, Matt. What will hitting him achieve?'

'It'll make me feel better.'

'But achieve nothing.'

For a moment the outcome hung in the balance, then he shrugged. 'You're right, of course. I'll be more usefully employed in getting the locks changed.' He took his mobile phone from his pocket. 'You can let go now.'

She kissed him, said, 'Thank you,' then turned back to confront the destruction, dropping to her knees to sift through the debris, hunting for something that she could save.

Amongst the dying leaves and scattered compost she found a crushed bud. It was split, bruised, but at its heart it was a clear primrose yellow.

'Matt?' She held it up, showed it to him.

'Which plant did it come from?'

'This one, I think.' She picked up the nearest ruin, reached for a pot, a handful of compost, trimmed off the top, set it on the bench. Then, because there was nothing else to do, she kept going, sorting through the remains to find what could be salvaged.

Behind her Matt called Sarah, asking her to come and fetch Tom and take him to school. He called the locksmith. When he put a call through to the police, she stopped him.

'Won't your insurance company insist?'

'The only damage is to the plants, Matt. And you can't insure a dream.'

'No.' He tossed the phone to one side and joined her, working beside her until every plant that looked as if it might be saved had been safely potted and restored to the bench. The day before they had been close to the peak of perfection, covered with fat buds, almost ready for the show bench.

Now they were sad remnants, little more than bare stalks, all their precious labels lost.

'We won't know what we've got until they come back into leaf and start flowering,' Fleur said when they surveyed their work.

'Somewhere amongst them there'll be a Gilbert's Gold,' he assured her.

'I'll have to ring the RHS and tell them we won't be at Chelsea.'

'Not this year, maybe, but plantsmen are nothing if not patient. Next year we'll be there,' Matt said, 'or the year after. Or the year after that.'

She turned to look at him. 'We?'

'We,' he repeated. 'You and me, Seth and my mother, Tom. Whatever happens, my love, we're in it together. It's taken the best part of a hundred and seventy-five years, but I think it's time that Gilbert and Hanover were reunited, partners again. What do you say?'

'Is that the idea you wanted to put to me?' she asked.

'What else?' And he smiled. 'Actually, I've already commissioned a sign painter to produce a new signboard.'

She sighed.

'What?'

'Nothing.' Then she admitted, 'I was just wishing I hadn't sold the barn. It was part of our history.'

'You really wish that?'

She looked up and realised that he was smiling.

'I was wondering what to give you for a wedding present. You've solved the problem.'

'What?'

'Martin and Lord didn't have a client. I bought the barn. I always hoped we could live there one day, and with my mother planning to convert her house into offices and a restaurant when she moves in with your father, we're going to need somewhere of our own.'

'You've got it all worked out, haven't you, Mr Hanover?'

'I still need you to say yes.'

She flung her arms around his neck and said, 'Yes, yes, yes!'

The entire village turned out to celebrate not just the blessing of Fleur and Matt Hanover's wedding, but to witness the union of Seth Gilbert and Katherine Hanover.

Everyone except Charlie Fletcher. No one had seen hide nor hair of him since the glasshouse had been wrecked. His house was empty and a For Sale sign had appeared in the garden. Fleur didn't ask Matt if he'd done anything to encourage him to move. There were some things she was probably better off not knowing.

Nothing, and no one was allowed to spoil a day of rejoicing that reunited the whole village in celebration. The Gilberts and the Hanovers erected a flower-bedecked marquee on the green, laid on enough food and drink to keep the whole village happy, and put on a celebration that would, as Matt had promised, be the talk of Longbourne for generations.

It took more than a year to convert the barn to the kind of home that attracted the attention of magazines who specialised in features on country life. The huge brick and beam structure had changed beyond recognition, as had the lives of the four members of the Gilbert-Hanover family who were finally going to move from 'Old Cottage' and take possession of their dream.

'Mummy, Daddy!' Tom came racing up the footpath from his grandparents' house clutching something in his fist. 'Grandad said I was to give you this.'

Fleur handed their baby daughter to Matt and crouched down to see what Tom was holding.

'What is it, sweetheart?'

He opened his hand and inside it, slightly squashed, lay a fat flower bud that had just split open to reveal its heart.

Pure gold.

If you enjoyed what you just read,
then we've got an offer you can't resist!

Take 2 bestselling
love stories FREE!
Plus get a FREE surprise gift!

Clip this page and mail it to Harlequin Reader Service®

IN U.S.A.	IN CANADA
3010 Walden Ave.	P.O. Box 609
P.O. Box 1867	Fort Erie, Ontario
Buffalo, N.Y. 14240-1867	L2A 5X3

YES! Please send me 2 free Harlequin Romance® novels and my free surprise gift. After receiving them, if I don't wish to receive anymore, I can return the shipping statement marked cancel. If I don't cancel, I will receive 6 brand-new novels every month, before they're available in stores! In the U.S.A., bill me at the bargain price of $3.57 plus 25¢ shipping & handling per book and applicable sales tax, if any*. In Canada, bill me at the bargain price of $4.05 plus 25¢ shipping & handling per book and applicable taxes**. That's the complete price and a savings of 10% off the cover prices—what a great deal! I understand that accepting the 2 free books and gift places me under no obligation ever to buy any books. I can always return a shipment and cancel at any time. Even if I never buy another book from Harlequin, the 2 free books and gift are mine to keep forever.

186 HDN DZ72
386 HDN DZ73

Name _____ (PLEASE PRINT)

Address _____ Apt.#

City _____ State/Prov. _____ Zip/Postal Code

Not valid to current Harlequin Romance® subscribers.
Want to try another series? Call 1-800-873-8635
or visit www.morefreebooks.com.

* Terms and prices subject to change without notice. Sales tax applicable in N.Y.
** Canadian residents will be charged applicable provincial taxes and GST.
  All orders subject to approval. Offer limited to one per household.
  ® are registered trademarks owned and used by the trademark owner or its licensee.

HROM04R   ©2004 Harlequin Enterprises Limited